When Life Gives You O.J.

Erica S. Perl

When Life Gives You O.J.

Alfred A. Knopf
New York

THIS IS A BORZOI BOOK PUBLISHED BY ALFRED A. KNOPF

Visit us on the Web! www.randomhouse.com/kids

Educators and librarians, for a variety of teaching tools, visit us at
www.randomhouse.com/teachers

Library of Congress Cataloging-in-Publication Data
Perl, Erica S.
When life gives you O.J. / by Erica S. Perl. — 1st ed.
p. cm.
Summary: Zelly Fried wants a dog more than anything, so at the urging of her grandfather, during the summer before sixth grade she takes care of a "practice dog" made out of an orange juice jug to show her parents that she is ready for the responsibility, even though she is sometimes not entirely sure about the idea.
ISBN 978-0-375-85924-3 (trade) — ISBN 978-0-375-95924-0 (lib. bdg.) —
ISBN 978-0-375-89783-2 (ebook)
[1. Grandfathers—Fiction. 2. Dogs—Fiction. 3. Family life—Vermont—Fiction.
4. Jews—United States—Fiction. 5. Self-confidence—Fiction. 6. Vermont—Fiction.] I. Title.
PZ7.P3163Wh 2011
[Fic]—dc22
2010023844

The text of this book is set in 12-point Goudy.

Printed in the United States of America
June 2011
10 9 8 7 6 5 4

First Edition

This book is dedicated to Sasha

When Life Gives You O.J.

CHAPTER 1

The whole mess started with a note:

> KID,
> SEE ME IMMEDIATELY WHEN YOU GET
> THIS. DO NOT SPEAK OF THIS TO ANYONE,
> NOT EVEN YOUR PARENTS OR YOUR
> BROTHER.
>
> ACE
> P.S. I HOPE YOU ARE READY FOR THIS.

I found the note on my nightstand, attached to a jug that definitely hadn't been there the night before. I had to put on my glasses to read it. On closer inspection, I could see that the jug was a plastic one, like the kind that milk comes in.

The note was attached to the neck of the jug with a green rubber band.

Even without his name on it, I would've known this was Ace's work. The rubber band was a dead giveaway. Ace is the proud owner of the world's largest rubber band collection. He doesn't trust Scotch tape.

Ready for what? I thought. I sat up in bed, staring at the jug. If Ace was behind this, I was definitely *not* ready for it.

Ace is my grandpa. His real name is Abraham Diamond, but he likes everyone to call him Ace. My name is Zelda Fried, but I like everyone to call me Zelly. Ace doesn't call me Zelly, or even Zelda. He calls me "kid," so I call him Grandpa to get him back.

I studied the note, then turned my attention to the jug. It was a big white plastic orange juice jug. Before Ace moved in with us, my mom always made pitchers of orange juice from small cans of frozen concentrate. Now she buys it premade in plastic jugs like this one because Ace drinks a lot of orange juice. He mixes scoops of powder into it, which he says keeps him "regular," whatever that means. Ace is about as far from a regular person as anyone could possibly be, and I can't imagine how any powder is going to change that.

I read the note again. *I HOPE YOU ARE READY FOR THIS*. I picked up the jug, which turned out to be empty, and unscrewed the bright orange cap. The faint scent of oranges wafted out.

Okay, fine, I thought, getting out of bed. *Let's go find out what this is all about.*

I left the jug where it was and went to the bathroom. The same owl eyes and freckle-strewn nose, framed by an especially frizzy halo of morning hair, stared back at me. I showed my teeth to make sure they were still, thankfully, pretty straight. When you already have crazy hair and glasses, the last thing you need is braces.

It seemed like everyone in the house was still asleep. Except maybe my little brother, Sam, who sometimes gets up super-early to build things in his room with his LEGOs or his blocks. He always forgets that when you wake up, you need to go pee, so after he's been building for about thirty minutes, he'll shoot down the hall to the bathroom.

I went back to my room and got the jug and the note. I carried them downstairs to Ace's room, which is also our TV room. Having the TV there makes my mom super-happy because Sam and I watch a lot less TV than we did a few months ago, when we lived in Brooklyn and the TV was in our living room. We practically never want to watch TV bad enough to hang out in Ace's room. True, Ace likes some of the same shows we do. For example, old *Star Trek* reruns. But he always ends up yelling at the TV so much that it isn't worth it.

I knocked quietly on Ace's door. No reply. The sign hanging on his door says GONE FISHING, but it's just for decoration. I don't think Ace has gone fishing once since we moved to Vermont and Ace moved in with us. GONE TO HENRY'S DINER

or GONE TO BEN & JERRY'S or GONE TO BATTERY PARK TO A BAND-SHELL CONCERT WEARING MY LUCKY FISHING HAT? Yes, yes, and yes. But GONE FISHING, not so much.

I looked at the jug. It didn't make any sense. Maybe Ace had finally completely flipped out. It seemed pretty likely. It occurred to me that maybe I should go upstairs and tell my parents. That thought made me feel all worried and nervous, though. What if Ace had gone crazy, and he got really mad at me for getting him in trouble? What if they dragged him off to the loony bin and he started yelling, *THIS IS ALL YOUR FAULT, KID!*

Which it kind of would be.

I took a deep breath and knocked again, harder this time. "Grandpa?" I called in a loudish whisper.

"WHA?" boomed Ace through the door.

"Grandpa," I whispered again. "It's me, Zelly."

"STOP WHISPERING ALREADY. I'M AWAKE. COME IN."

I entered the room and immediately tripped on something and fell flat on my face. I had a feeling it had been one of Ace's many pairs of golf shoes. That's another thing about Ace. He stopped playing golf years ago, but he loved the shoes so much that he started wearing them all the time. He probably has about twenty pairs. If anyone asks about his shoes, he launches into this lecture about how they "give excellent arch support."

"WHO'S THERE?" yelled Ace. I was on all fours, feeling my way over to the wall, where I knew there was a light

switch. I had dropped the jug when I fell. Before I could make it very far, Ace switched his bedside lamp on.

"WHAT IN THE NAME OF—?" said Ace.

"Sorry," I said. "I just tripped, and, I mean, I got your note."

"NOTE? WHAT NOTE?"

Okay, he's definitely gone crazy, I thought to myself. *Just back up and out and go see Mom and Dad.* But there's something about the way Ace talks. His voice practically requires an answer.

"The note you, uh, put on the orange juice jug?" I spotted the jug lying on its side on the floor, but I left it where it was. Instead, I walked over to Ace and handed him the note.

"OH," said Ace, putting on his glasses and swinging his legs out of bed. He looked it over carefully, as if seeing it for the first time. "THAT NOTE."

"Uh-huh," I said, getting ready to make my exit.

"SO?"

"Sorry?"

"SO, ARE YOU?"

"Am I what?"

"ARE YOU READY?"

"Ready for what?"

Ace looked exasperated with me. "DO YOU WASH YOUR EARS WITH CHOPPED LIVER? READY TO GET A DOG, FOR CRYING OUT LOUD!"

"Oh! I mean, of course," I said.

Beyond ready was what I thought. I had been begging my

parents to let me get a dog for years, and especially since April, when we moved to Vermont and Ace moved in with us. I am, to put it mildly, a dog lover. Okay, I'll admit it: I am obsessed with dogs. All of my notebooks have dogs on the cover and are filled with dog doodles. I cut the *Dogs, Cats, Pets* column out of the newspaper almost every day, and I've read every dog book ever written (*Shiloh* is my favorite). In three months, Ace had probably heard me ask about getting a dog at least three zillion times.

But what did that have to do with the jug? Or Ace's mysterious note?

Ace smiled. He put one hand on his bedside table and lifted himself out of bed. He took the cane that he was supposed to use but never did and turned it around so the hook side was pointed at the ground. Then, using the cane, he hooked the handle of the orange juice jug, picked it up, and carried it over to me. I unhooked it from the end of the cane.

"KID," said Ace, "MEET YOUR NEW DOG."

I stood there, holding the jug and staring at him. I knew crazy people sometimes heard voices in their heads or saw things that other people couldn't see. Did Ace think there was a dog there in the room with us?

"Um, where?" I asked.

Ace reached out and thumped the orange juice jug with his hand.

"RIGHT THERE. YOU'RE HOLDING HIM."

"I . . . This?" I held out the jug with both hands to make

sure I understood what he was saying. "You think this is a dog?"

"NO, FOR CRYING OUT LOUD. WHAT KIND OF A MESHUGGENER DO YOU THINK I AM?"

Meshuggener is the Yiddish word for "a crazy person." Ace says it a lot when he reads the *New York Times*. Also when he watches the news on TV. According to him, most politicians are meshuggeners. He also thinks Captain Kirk acts like a meshuggener. Especially when he gets himself beamed down onto planets without checking them out first.

"No, Grandpa, I just . . . I'm sorry, I don't understand."

"ENOUGH WITH THE 'SORRY.' VEY IZ MIR, KID." Ace shook his head. Clearly, he was disappointed in me. Ace lapses into extra Yiddish when he wants to make a point, which is often. He'll say *Oy vey!* Or *Vey iz mir!* which is like an *Oy vey!* and then some. He pointed to the jug and spoke slowly.

"THIS," he said, "IS NOT A DOG. OKAY?"

"Okay," I said.

"IT'S NOT A DOG, SO WHAT IS IT?" he demanded.

"Um, it's an orange juice jug?"

"WRONG!" yelled Ace. "THIS IS NOT AN ORANGE JUICE JUG. THIS IS YOUR NEW PRACTICE DOG. THIS IS WHAT YOU USE TO SHOW YOUR PARENTS THAT YOU ARE RESPONSIBLE ENOUGH TO GET A REAL DOG."

"Practice dog?" I asked.

"RIGHT! EVERYTHING YOU DO FOR A REAL DOG, YOU DO FOR THE PRACTICE DOG."

"Yeah, but Grandpa, you can't do dog things with an orange juice jug."

"IT'S NOT AN ORANGE JUICE JUG. DON'T CALL IT AN ORANGE JUICE JUG! I TOLD YOU, IT'S A PRACTICE DOG."

"Okay, well, how do you walk a practice dog? It doesn't have any legs."

Ace smiled like he had been waiting for this question. He went over to his bedside table and opened the drawer. Out of it he brought a long nylon leash with a metal ring on one end. He threaded it through the handle of the jug and put the nylon hand loop at one end through the ring at the other. He then pulled the leash tight and let go.

"WHAT DO YOU DO WITH A DOG THAT HAS NO LEGS?"

"Sorry?"

"I TOLD YOU, KID, ENOUGH WITH THE 'SORRY'! WHAT YOU DO WITH A DOG THAT HAS NO LEGS IS, YOU TAKE HIM OUT FOR A DRAG."

"You what?"

"IT'S A JOKE. BUT WITH YOUR PRACTICE DOG, THAT'S WHAT YOU DO. TWO, MAYBE THREE TIMES A DAY, YOU PUT ON HIS LEASH AND TAKE HIM FOR HIS WALK."

"Outside?"

"OF COURSE OUTSIDE. UNLESS YOU WANT HIM TO DO HIS BUSINESS IN THE HOUSE."

"His business? An orange juice jug can't—"

"LOOK, KID. THIS IS NOT GOING TO WORK IF YOU KEEP SAYING ORANGE JUICE JUG. PRACTICE. DOG."

"A *practice dog* can't go to the bathroom."

Ace smiled again. He went back to his bedside table and opened a drawer. He returned carrying a bag of dog food.

"WANNA BET?" he said.

Ace went on to explain to me how a practice dog worked. Every morning, I would take my practice dog down to break- fast with me. I would pour water into the neck of the ju— *practice dog* and then add a couple of spoonfuls of dry dog food. After breakfast, I would put the leash on and take the practice dog out for a walk. At some point on the walk, I would unscrew the cap and pour out the contents to let the practice dog relieve himself. Then I would take a plastic bag—which I would bring along on the walk—and use it to scoop up the wet pile of *practice* doggy doo and get rid of it. I would do the same thing for the practice dog's dinner and evening walk.

"You said three walks a day. What's the third walk for?" I asked, immediately realizing that I probably shouldn't have brought it up.

"THAT'S THE AFTERNOON WALK. FOR EXER- CISE," said Ace.

"Exercise?" I pictured myself throwing a stick, then dragging the jug to "fetch" it.

"EXERCISE," repeated Ace firmly. Case closed.

"Okay, so how long do I have to do this?"

"YOU HAVEN'T EVEN STARTED DOING YOUR PART OF OUR PLAN YET AND ALREADY YOU'RE KVETCHING AND HOCKING ME ABOUT WHEN CAN YOU STOP?"

"I'm not kvetching or hocking you," I protested. I knew *kvetching* was Yiddish for "complaining," and I was pretty sure *hocking* meant "nagging." "I just want to know how long this might— Wait a second. *'Our plan'*?"

I suddenly remembered a conversation I'd had with Ace several days before. It was after dinner and after another argument with my parents about getting a dog. I was in my room rereading *Shiloh* when Ace shuffled in.

"LOOK, KID," Ace had announced. "YOU'RE GOING ABOUT THIS ALL WRONG."

"Thanks," I said, without looking up from my book. I had no idea what he was talking about, but it was fairly common for Ace to get an opinion in his head and need to bombard someone with it.

"I KNOW THIS STUFF," continued Ace. "IN ALL MY YEARS ON THE BENCH, I'VE SEEN A LOT OF LAWYERS." *On the bench* meant "being a judge," which was a major basis for Ace's authority on many topics. "YOU KNOW WHAT YOUR PROBLEM IS, KID? YOU ARE ONE LOUSY LAWYER."

"Thanks," I said again. I hoped that when he noticed I wasn't arguing with him, he'd get bored and leave.

"YOU DON'T HAVE TO THANK ME, KID." Ace grinned. "BUT TELL YOU WHAT: I'M GONNA DO YOU A FAVOR."

"Uh, no thanks," I said quickly. A "favor" from Ace usually involved him telling you a long story or an unfunny joke. I wasn't in the mood for either one.

"YOU WANT A DOG?"

"What?" I put down my book.

"DO YOU WANT A DOG?"

"Yes."

"SO? YOU WANT A DOG, YOU LISTEN TO ME. I HAVE A PLAN TO GET YOU A DOG."

Ace looked pretty crazy all of a sudden. Crazier than usual. His caterpillar eyebrows were all tufted up, and his eyes were kind of twitching with excitement.

"Grandpa, look. If you just bring home a dog, they're not going to let me keep it."

Ace waved his hands at me like I was the one talking crazy.

"WHAT KIND OF A SHMENDRICK DO YOU THINK I AM? I DIDN'T SAY, 'BRING HOME A DOG.' I SAID"— and now he talked even louder and pronounced each word extra-clearly, like I was the one with the hearing aid—"A PLAN TO GET YOU A DOG. A PLAN TO MAKE IT SO YOUR PARENTS LET YOU GET A DOG."

"Okay," I said, becoming curious. "How?"

Ace smiled with satisfaction, like he had just told one of his famously bad jokes. "ARE YOU IN?"

"I guess."

"OH NO. YOU CAN'T GUESS. IF YOU'RE IN, YOU'RE IN. YOU GOTTA DO WHAT I SAY TO DO, WHEN I SAY TO DO IT. EVEN IF YOU DON'T WANT TO, YOU GOTTA STICK WITH THE PLAN AS LONG AS IT TAKES. NO MATTER WHAT. SO DON'T SAY YOU'RE IN IF YOU'RE NOT IN. IT'S ALL OR NOTH-ING, KID."

"Okay, okay."

"OKAY, WHAT?"

"Okay, I'm in."

Ace clapped his hands together once, loudly. Then he held out his right hand to me like a businessman. I shook it and was surprised at how strong his grip was underneath his loose, spotted old-person skin.

"So . . . what do I do?" I asked eagerly.

"BUPKIS," said Ace.

I frowned. "Nothing?" I asked. Was this some sort of joke?

"ZORG ZIKH NISHT."

"Zug . . . what?"

"DON'T WORRY," he explained.

"I'm not worried," I said. "It's just—"

"SO, ALL RIGHT, ALREADY. ALL IN GOOD TIME, KID. TO THOSE WHO WAIT SHALL COME ALL THE RICHES OF THE WORLD."

And with that he walked out, leaving me more confused

than when he came in. To be fair, it felt like something momentous had just taken place. But the next morning, nothing. And the next, and the next. So I sort of forgot about it.

Until now. Until the jug appeared.

"SHE WANTS TO KNOW HOW LONG THIS MIGHT TAKE?" said Ace. "AS LONG AS IT NEEDS TO, KID. AND NOT ONE MINUTE LONGER."

I looked at Ace. I looked at the jug.

I had a feeling this was going to take a long time.

Chapter 2

"Please pass the O.J.," sang Sam for the fourth time.

"Ha-ha," I said.

Sam giggled. "Oops! I mean, please pass the dog! I mean O.J.! I mean dog! I mean O.J.!"

"Sam," said my mother lightly, though she was smiling too. When Ace had demonstrated how to feed my practice dog and announced to my parents that I was going to start caring for "it," it was clear that they found the whole idea very amusing.

"Having a plastic dog will definitely cut down on vet bills," said my dad. "And no barking, either. This sounds like the kind of dog that I could really get behind." He patted the orange juice jug on the cap, like you'd pat a dog's head. "What breed did you say it was, again?"

"Dad!" I said. This wasn't supposed to be a joke. I wondered if it had occurred to Ace that my parents might like the "practice dog" so much, they wouldn't want to replace it with a real, live dog. A real, live, barking, running-up-vet-bills dog.

"Who wants French toast?" asked my mom, changing the subject. "I think we've got some leftover challah around here somewhere."

"I want green," yelled Sam, who only eats French toast and pancakes if my parents add food coloring.

"Zell, you in?" asked my mom.

"Only if it's not green."

My mom sighed loudly. "Just once, it would be nice not to have to dirty *two* pans." But she got out two pie plates and began breaking eggs into each.

"Where should I put it?" I asked Ace, once I had fed the "dog."

"WHAT 'IT'?"

"The, you know, this." I picked up the jug. I still couldn't bring myself to call it a dog.

"SO, NU?" said Ace, using one of his favorite Yiddish expressions, which basically meant "So, what's up?" "YOU HAVEN'T NAMED IT YET?"

"Named it?" I asked, hoping he was kidding.

"WHO EVER HEARD OF A DOG WITH NO NAME? I HEARD OF A DOG WITH NO NOSE ONCE. YOU KNOW HOW HE SMELLED?"

"No," I said.

"TERRIBLE!" roared Ace. My dad smirked like he had

heard the joke before. Sam looked confused for a second. Then, all of a sudden, he started to laugh.

"I get it. He smelled! Like P.U.!" said Sam, pinching his nose. "Right, Ace?"

"RIGHT YOU ARE, SAMMY, MY BOY." Ace beamed with pleasure, hiking his pants up even higher over his belly. Then, with no warning, he started to cough. And cough. And cough. Sammy's eyes got huge, the way they always do when Ace starts sounding like he's going to hack up a lung. Ace held up one finger, still coughing, in a "Remain calm" gesture.

"You okay, Dad?" said my mom, patting Ace on the back.

Ace nodded vigorously, still coughing but also scowling like she was crazy. "I'M FINE," he insisted when he finally stopped. Then he pulled out his handkerchief, blew his nose into it—*PFFFFFFFTTT!!!*—and calmly stuck it back into his pocket. Yuck! He ran his brown-speckled hands across the top of his head, almost as if he was trying to find his hair, before locating what's left of it in small frizzy tufts around his ears. He made useless attempts to smooth them before adjusting the big, round glasses that make his caterpillar eyebrows look even more gigantic.

"I'M AS FIT AS A FIDDLER CRAB," he added, snapping his hand like a crab claw and winking at Sam. Sam, who is convinced he's the world's greatest winker, blinked back.

"SPEAKING OF WHICH," continued Ace, making a mischievous face that could mean only one thing: fish-joke alert. Ace is a big fan of fish jokes. Bad fish jokes in particular. Before I could even start my eyes rolling, Ace demanded,

"WHAT'S GREEN, HANGS ON THE WALL, AND WHISTLES?"

"I don't know," said Sammy, even though he does know because, like me, he's heard the joke about a thousand times before. But this is what you're supposed to say, and Sammy loves to play his part.

"A HERRING!" Ace answered proudly. Then Sam, grinning just as goofily as Ace, said his next line, which is "But a herring isn't green!" Which is dumb because who knows what color a herring is? I know it is a fish because my dad told me, but that's about it.

So Sam said, "But a herring isn't green," and Ace answered, "YOU PAINT IT GREEN." And he shrugged like Sam was being ridiculous. Sam's next line was "But a herring doesn't hang on the wall!" (When Ace tries to rope me into the herring joke, I sometimes try to skip this bit. "IT'S PART OF THE JOKE. GO ON!" demands Ace.) It would never cross Sam's mind to skip any part, of course, and as soon as he said it, Ace answered, "YOU NAIL IT THERE!" Then Sam did his last line, which is "But a herring doesn't whistle."

Ace grinned like crazy, and his caterpillar eyebrows hopped up and down in place. "I JUST THREW THAT IN TO MAKE IT HARDER," he said triumphantly.

Sam beamed, thrilled to be part of Ace's act. I shook my head, knowing that Sam's enthusiasm would only make Ace more likely to tell the joke than ever. "AND SPEAKING OF HERRING," continued Ace, "DID I EVER TELL YOU THE ONE ABOUT THE SHMENDRICK . . . ," and

he launched into another of his stories. Thankfully, not a fish one, but still.

"Hey, that's it!" yelled Sam. "Zelly, you should call him 'Shmendrick'!"

"Or maybe I should call him 'Shut Up'?" I replied. Sam's comment made me think of Nicky Benoit, the boy in my class who started picking on me the minute I moved to Vermont. He was going to have a field day if he ever found out about my "practice dog."

"Zelda," said my mom warningly.

"What? It was just an idea for the name."

"How about Spot?" suggested my dad in his *Kids, no fighting* voice.

"Great, except there's no spot on it," I informed him, showing him the jug.

"You could paint one on?" said my dad, winking at my mom. It sounded like he was telling one of Ace's jokes.

"This isn't funny!" I said, my voice getting shrill.

"Okay, okay, you're right. I'm sorry," said my dad.

"I've got one," said my mom, carrying a piece of normal-colored challah French toast on a spatula. She deposited it on my plate, then passed me the syrup. "How about 'O.J.'?"

"O.J.?" I asked. "Like *orange juice?*"

"Right," said my mom. "It sounds like a dog's name, doesn't it? *Good boy, O.J. Fetch the paper, O.J.*"

"Well, fetching may not be one of this dog's strong suits," remarked my dad. "Seeing how he is, shall we say, a little challenged in the leg department."

"Okay, fine," I said. "O.J. it is." I put the jug down on the floor next to my chair and reached for the maple syrup. I poured a pool of syrup onto my plate for dipping. More than anything, I just wanted to stop talking about the dumb old jug. *Hey, that's it,* I realized suddenly, perking up at the thought. *O.J.* didn't have to stand for "Orange Juice." It could also stand for "Old Jug." *Dumb* Old Jug, that is.

"Good boy, O.J.!" said Sam, leaning down to pat my "dog" on the "head."

"Watch out," I informed him. "O.J. bites."

After breakfast, my parents started bustling around the kitchen, packing stuff up. Their plan for the day was for all of us to go on a family outing to pick cherries.

"Why do we have to go, again?" I asked.

"Remember how Mrs. Stanley told us about this?"

I shook my head. Mrs. Stanley is our next-door neighbor. She's always telling my mom about great Vermont places to go and things to see. But she has a super-cute, super-old beagle named Bridget, so most of the time I just pay attention to Bridget and tune Mrs. Stanley out.

My mom explained, "There's a cherry orchard just outside of town, but they have a very short season. Really just a couple of days, apparently."

"So, maybe we already missed it?"

My mom smiled. "Why don't we go and find out?"

"I have an idea. You guys could go cherry picking, and I could go over to Al—" I almost said "Allie's" out of habit. But

unfortunately, for another two whole weeks, my best friend in the entire world would still be at sleepaway camp. I swallowed hard. ". . . Reesa's?" I suggested.

"It's Saturday. Doesn't she have swim meets every weekend?"

"Uh . . . maybe." I had forgotten about that. "What about Tasha and Talia?" I hadn't seen the twins since school let out, but it would be much more fun than—

"I believe their mom said they were spending most of July on the Cape. Besides, Zell, this is family time."

I sighed. My parents are big on "family time," especially on weekend mornings. When I was Sam's age, I didn't mind so much because sometimes family time meant *ice cream*. But now that I'm almost eleven, I'd rather hang out with my friends, even if it means there's no ice cream.

"Not for every family," I said, looking down at my feet and thinking, *Not for Allie's family*. It felt like she had been gone for a million years and wouldn't be back for a million more.

"Oh, sweetie, chin up," said my mom, putting a hand on my shoulder. "I'm sure you'll hear from Allie soon."

Hear from Allie. That would be good. Not that it would be anywhere near as good as if I had gotten to go, or if she was home now, but at least it would be *something*.

"What time does the mail come?" I asked.

"Zelly, you ask me that every day. Late afternoon. It will probably be here when we get back from cherry picking. Now come on, go get dressed. Chop-chop!"

"There should be a law against best friends being separated in the summer," I said.

My mom looked amused. "You sound just like your grandfather," she said.

My parents said the same thing when I tried to convince them to send me to sleepaway camp with Allie in the first place. I had made a list of the reasons why I should be allowed to go, which I read out loud to them.

Top Five Reasons I Should Get To Go To Camp Sonrise With Allie

1. We're best friends and best friends shouldn't be separated. Especially not in summer.
2. Allie says it's not expensive.
3. They have drama and archery and lots of fun outdoor activities.
4. I'm practically eleven.
5. Julia can look out for us.

Julia is Allie's big sister. Usually, she either ignores us or bosses us around, but I figured my parents might not need to know that.

"Um, Zell," said my mom, "those are all good reasons, and it's great that you wrote them all out and made such a good case for them."

"Good advocacy skills run in the family," said my dad.

"But it's not that simple. I mean, it's just . . . ," said my mom, looking at my dad for help.

"What your mother means is . . . ," started my dad.

"The camp Allie and her sister go to," said my mom, "is, well—"

"IT'S FOR THE GOYIM," interrupted Ace, who had been listening from across the room. Ace wears a hearing aid, and I guess he must turn it up when he wants to hear stuff from far away. He must not be able to hear his own voice all that well, though, because he always talks in a booming voice, much louder than anyone else.

"Dad!" said my mom.

"WHAT? IT'S TRUE. WHAT'S THE BIG DEAL?"

"What's 'the goyim'?" I asked.

"It means 'non-Jewish people,'" said my dad.

"What's wrong with non-Jewish people?"

"Nothing!" said my mom and dad together.

"Do you have something against non-Jewish people?" I asked them suspiciously.

"Of course not," said my mom, glaring at Ace.

"Then why can't I go?"

"Sweetie," said my mom, "that camp is run by a church. So a lot of the activities are church-related. Church songs, church crafts—"

"MAKING FUDGE," added Ace.

"Dad!" snapped my mom.

"What does that mean?" I asked him.

Ace shrugged. "IT'S A PROVEN FACT: JEWS CAN'T

MAKE FUDGE. THE GOYIM, THEY KNOW HOW TO MAKE FUDGE."

"Well, what if I want to learn how to make fudge? They can't tell me I can't go just because I'm Jewish, right?"

"That's not really the point," said my mom.

"Then why can't I go?"

"Well, for starters, you're not eleven yet," said my dad, shooting my mom one of his *Let's take this down a notch* looks.

"I'm almost eleven. I'm going into sixth grade, just like Allie."

"Look, Zellybelly," he said, "it's been a pretty zany couple of months, what with the move and"—he glanced at Ace— "everything else. The way your mom and I see it, this summer is a good time for all of us to just slow down and settle in."

"But I'm already settled in," I told him. "And while I'm off at camp, you guys can slow down all you want." I gave one more pleading look and crossed my fingers on both hands.

"Maybe next summer, sweetie," offered my mom, "we can look at some sleepaway camps for you."

"That's a thought," agreed my dad, like this solved everything.

When Allie called later that night, I told her what had happened.

"Bring me back some fudge, okay?" I said.

"We get to make fudge?" she asked. "Julia never said anything about fudge."

"Yeah, well, maybe it's one of those camp secrets."

"It's not fair," said Allie. "I don't want to go if you can't go."

"Maybe you can stay home," I suggested.

"Hey, yeah!" said Allie. "Oh, except my parents are having our kitchen renovated while we're gone, so they're staying with my aunt."

"You could stay with me," I offered. "A three-week sleepover! How good would that be?"

"The best!" said Allie. But then she was quiet, probably because she was thinking the same thing as me: *No way are my parents going to go for that.*

"Well, if they make you go anyway," I finally said, "you have to promise you won't get a new best friend there."

"Yeah, well, duh! You neither."

"Oh, right. Like who? Nicky Benoit?"

"I think I'm gonna hurl," said Allie.

I replied by making noises like Allie's cat makes when it's going to be sick: *ulp, ulp, ulp.*

Allie laughed. Then she said, "Hey, I know! I have Julia's old camp trunk. We could hide you in it."

"Yeah! I'll just curl up real tiny," I said.

"Exactly! And I'll put all my towels and camp stuff over you to hide you. . . ."

"And we can poke some holes in the side. . . ."

"Yeah, and pack snacks and stuff. . . ."

"And then by the time anyone finds out, it'll be too late."

"Yeah!" I felt a rush of excitement. "It's a plan."

Even though we were just kidding around, the day before camp started, we actually tried to see if I'd fit in her trunk. Even with most of the clothes pulled out, and my knees tucked up under my chin, it didn't quite work.

"Take your shoes off," suggested Allie, standing over me.

"O-kay?" I said carefully, because my head was pretty tightly wedged in. I shifted a little onto my back and stuck one foot in the air. Allie was pulling my shoes off for me when Julia walked in.

"What are you two—"

"Nothing!" we yelled. I unwedged my head and sat up, embarrassed.

"A stowaway?" Julia looked amused.

"NO!" protested Allie. Piles of her shorts, T-shirts, and bathing suits surrounded the camp trunk. In which I was sitting.

"Here's an idea," suggested Julia. "Why don't you just *sign up for camp?*"

"My parents," I said.

"Oh," said Julia, nodding knowledgeably.

"It's so unfair!" said Allie.

"Yeah, whatever." Julia shrugged. "It's not for everyone."

"What are you talking about?" asked Allie. "You love camp."

"Yeah," said Julia. "But Zelly might not."

"Well, I'm not going if Zelly can't go!" insisted Allie, looking at me.

"Yeah, you are," said Julia, laughing.

Allie shook her head, folded her arms, and planted her feet. I nodded back, equally defiant. I could tell we were both thinking the exact same thing.

She just had to get a bigger trunk.

Unfortunately, Allie's parents didn't get her a bigger trunk. Julia's old trunk—and Allie—left for camp the next day. Without me. So while I was stuck getting ready for "family time" picking cherries, she was probably doing drama or computer clubhouse or making fudge . . . or who knows what else? I didn't know because I hadn't gotten a single letter from her yet.

I've always loved getting mail, and I was pretty sure Allie knew it. The first time she ever passed me a note in class, she wrote "Special Delivery" on the outside, and drew lines to make the folded-up paper look like a tiny envelope. I couldn't help wondering, *Why hasn't she written to me from camp?*

Back when we still lived in New York, my grandma, Bubbles, sent me letters all the time. She was a painter, so she wrote on sketchbook paper with little doodles crowding out the words. The letter I remember best was actually a birthday card she made for me for my third or fourth birthday. It had an enormous giraffe drawn on the front. My eyes must have gotten huge when I saw the giraffe sticking its long neck under our apartment door. My mom picked it up and read out loud, "'I came a looooooong way. . . .'" Then she opened the card and read, "'just to see you today.'" And then the doorbell rang, and there was Bubbles herself, squatted

down to my height, her arms open as wide as her smile. "Surprise!" she crowed. For years I was convinced that Bubbles had stamped herself, climbed into a mailbox, and mailed herself to me.

Walking upstairs to get dressed for cherry picking, I pictured Allie sitting on my doorstep, her forehead covered in stamps. Okay, not very likely, but the thought cheered me up. As did the thought that a letter might come today. But the thing was, I thought the same thing every morning when I woke up, and every afternoon I'd jump at the sound of the mail slot only to find: no letter. *Still, maybe today will be the day*, I told myself, trying to shake off the nervous feeling that my best friend in the whole wide world had completely forgotten about me.

When I got downstairs, I almost tripped on something blocking the front door.

The Dumb Old Jug.

Hooked to its handle was the leash.

Underneath it was a plastic bag.

And rubber-banded to its neck was a new note.

This note said:

> I NEED MY MORNING WALK.
> YOU MIGHT NOT BE BACK IN TIME FOR MY
> AFTERNOON WALK TOO, SO YOU NEED TO
> TAKE ME ALONG.
> EXERCISE, REMEMBER?
>
> O.J.

I groaned. "You've got to be kidding me," I said.

Outside, the car horn honked twice.

I grabbed the handle of the Dumb Old Jug, the leash trailing behind, and went outside, slamming the door behind me.

"Can you wait a sec?" I asked my mom. "I've gotta, uh, walk the Dumb Old— Uh, I mean, O.J."

My mom looked irritated. "Didn't you take care of that already?"

"I'm hot!" whined Sam from the backseat.

"Close your window, Sam," said my dad, "I've got the air conditioning on." He leaned across my mom and told me, "Hurry."

"Okay," I said. I put the Dumb Old Jug down and dragged it across the driveway to the grass edging our walk. I unscrewed the cap and upturned the jug.

A thin stream of watery brown liquid trickled out.

But nothing else.

I looked into the jug. Brownish, dog-food-colored gunk was firmly stuck to the bottom of the jug.

My whole family stared at me, along with our neighbor Mrs. Brownell, who was coming around the corner walking her poodles, Maddy and Luna. Ordinarily, I'd run over to say hi and pet them. But right now I had my hands more than a little full.

"Come ON!" I said through clenched teeth, shaking the jug. I smacked the bottom of it with one hand. Luna perked

up her ears at the sound, like she thought it might mean she was about to get a treat.

The weight inside the jug shifted, and a small, wet blob fell out. At first, I thought it was a brown marshmallow, but then I realized it was a nugget of dog food, only swollen to twice its size. With several additional smacks, more wet, messy lumps came rolling out. Eventually, most of what was inside the jug plopped itself out onto the ground, forming a disgusting-looking soggy brown pile.

Ugh.

Across the street, Luna pulled hard on her leash, like she was dying to meet the new "dog." Determinedly, she started to drag Mrs. Brownell and Maddy over for a visit. Maddy didn't look so thrilled. She began to bark.

I took out the bag and quickly tried to use it to pick up the sloppy pile of pretend dog poop. On my first try, I got some—but nowhere near all—of it into the bag. Using a stick, I tried to push more of the mess into the bag. All this did was get the outside of the bag muddy and rip a hole in it.

"Zelly?" My mom had rolled down her window. "Could you hurry it up? Please?"

I stared at her in disbelief. What did she think I was doing? With frantic prodding, a tiny bit more of the mess made its way into the now-leaking bag.

"I'm done, all right?" I said, just as Mrs. Brownell approached, talking to me and the dogs at once. "Hello, Zelda, dear! Luna, stop pulling! Maddy, for heaven's sake, be quiet!"

I turned to toss the bag in the trash can before Mrs. Brownell could see what I was doing. But I forgot that I had left the Dumb Old Jug right behind me. I lowered my foot, but I kind of half stepped on O.J., who was empty, so he went flying forward.

"Rrrrowf! Arr, arr, arr!" Maddy went haywire.

"Wurf! Wurf! Wurf!" Luna chimed in with her squeaky little barks, skittering toward O.J.

Everything happened fast. I leaned forward to grab O.J., but Luna's leash tripped me, making me stumble and almost land on her, so I stepped backward—

"Whoops—" and tripped over Maddy—

"Waaah—" and tried not to fall—

"Whoa—" and sat down—

Oof—

—right in the middle of what was left of O.J.'s poop.

Maddy stopped barking. She sniffed where I was sitting for about half a second.

Then she began to chow down.

"Maddy! NO! Bad girl!" said Mrs. Brownell, trying to pull her off. "I am *so* sorry!"

"It's okay," I told her, trying to stand up and get out of the mushy pile. One of my flip-flops slid off, stuck. "It's not what it looks like," I tried to explain to her.

Mrs. Brownell told me she understood completely. But just then she remembered she had left something on the stove, so she set off down the block, pulling a disappointed Luna and a still-barking Maddy behind her.

"HEY, KID," said Ace, who had come out of the house and was standing on the front step watching me. "THAT'S WHAT THE BAG IS FOR."

"I know that!" I told him.

Ace put on his lucky fishing hat and walked past me to the car.

"COULDA FOOLED ME," he said.

CHAPTER 3

I gotta say, sitting in a pile of wet, smelly dog poop—even if it was fake dog poop—pretty much convinced me that the deal I made with Ace was a bad one. Luckily, my mom found me a clean pair of shorts and hosed down my flip-flops while I changed. We left to go cherry picking before I got the chance to tell Ace that the deal was off. The whole way there, Ace entertained Sam with one of his famous long-winded fishing stories. This one was about the fishing contest he once had with his old friend Charlie O'Brien.

"AND, WOULD YOU BELIEVE IT? AFTER FIVE HOURS ON THE WATER, CHARLIE AND I ARE NECK AND NECK, MATCHED—"

"Fish to fish," said Sam.

"FISH TO FISH!" echoed Ace. "WHEN ALL OF A

SUDDEN, KABLOOIE!" Ace smacked the armrest on the car door for emphasis. "OUT OF THE BLUE, THIS CRAZY FISH COMES FLYING AT ME! NO HOOK, NO NOTHING, THIS ONE. JUST PLAIN HURLING ITSELF OUT OF THE WATER INTO MY LAP."

"And not just any fish!" added Sam.

"AND NOT JUST ANY FISH," continued Ace, "THE MOST MESHUGGE FISH IN THE SEA. A SEA ROBIN! SO WHAT DID I DO, YOU MIGHT ASK?"

"So what did you do?" asked Sam, on cue.

Sam never gets tired of Ace's fish stories. I do. The O'Briens were my grandparents' neighbors back when they used to live in Brooklyn, right near us. Every time I'd be over at my grandparents' apartment and we'd run into the O'Briens, Mr. O'Brien would say to me, "Tell that grandfather of yours I'm going to have him arrested for fish fraud!" Ace would bellow back, "QUIT YOUR CARPING!" Bubbles would always shake her head. "You two get more pleasure out of kvetching about those fish than you did catching them," she'd say.

Ace kept right on going, through the climactic part about how Charlie had a fish on his line at the time but then suddenly a sea robin—which is this weird, ugly fish with legs like a lobster and wings like a bat—jumped into the boat and onto Ace's lap, startling Charlie so much he dropped his rod and *his* fish slipped off the hook. Ace was almost at the part where he kissed the sea robin triumphantly.

"How come Charlie didn't win?" I interrupted.

Ace stopped midstory, turned, and stared at me. This wasn't in the script. We were supposed to say our parts at the right times, or keep quiet and listen.

"HOW COME WHAT?" he said.

My heart beat faster, and I began talking to match it. "The contest was for catching fish, right? Like with a fishing rod. You didn't catch that sea robin. It just sort of landed on you. So it shouldn't count."

Ace studied me. "YOU ARE SUGGESTING IT WAS A TIE?" he asked slowly.

"No," I said, feeling dangerous. "I am suggesting that Charlie won. Because he actually hooked one more fish than you did."

Ace was silent. For a second he was going to congratulate me for making a good point. But then I saw my dad glance nervously in the rearview mirror.

"NOT BEING A FISHERMAN," Ace started, "YOU MAY NOT REALIZE THAT *CATCH* IS IN FACT A TERM OF ART. WHEREAS . . ."

As soon as he said the word *whereas*, I knew I was sunk. My dad had warned me about this shortly after we moved to Vermont and Ace started living with us. The subject came up because of Ace's beloved golf shoe collection. His golf shoes had spikes on the bottom, so they left these little polka dot prints all over the living room carpet and made clicking noises on the kitchen floor. Every time my mom would remind Ace to leave his golf shoes at the door, Ace would launch into

a lecture about arch support. Finally, my dad solved the problem by getting this tool for unscrewing the spikes.

"I am the Zen master," said my dad proudly after Ace walked off, happy yet spikeless. "Let this be a lesson to you, kids. Never argue with your grandfather."

"Why not?" I asked. My mom says that the fact that my dad doesn't enjoy arguing is one of the reasons she married him. But, unlike my dad, sometimes I can't help it.

"Because," said my dad, "Ace has high blood pressure, and when he argues, it gets elevated, which is not good for his health. Besides, with Ace, you will never win."

"But what if—" I started to ask, but my dad raised a hand to stop me.

"You will *never* win," he repeated.

Sure enough, Ace went from *whereas* to the rules, the regulations, and what he called the "social morays" of fishing. By the time he was finished, I felt like a total idiot for suggesting that there was any doubt in anyone's mind that Ace had won the fishing contest, fair and square.

"Morays?" asked Sam. "Like a moray eel?"

Ace stared at Sam for a long moment. Then he broke into a smile and let out a huge belly laugh. He put one arm around Sam's shoulder and gave him noogies with the other while Sam protested, chortling with laughter.

It was official. Ace loved Sam, and Bubbles loved me.

Boy, did I miss Bubbles.

Bubbles became Bubbles when I was a baby because I got *bubbe*, the Yiddish word for "grandma," and *bubbles*, like in a bath, all mixed up and it stuck. When I was little, Bubbles and Ace lived in Brooklyn, right near us. But when Ace retired "from the bench," he and Bubbles surprised everyone by announcing they were moving to Vermont. I guess it was so they could have more space and Bubbles could have a real art studio. Bubbles loved Vermont and claimed the light there was better for her painting. "And there's no traffic, and not so much noise," she used to say, for Ace's benefit. Ace often replied, "SO WHAT AM I SUPPOSED TO KVETCH ABOUT NOW? THE COWS?" "You'll think of something," teased Bubbles.

Bubbles and Ace's house in Vermont was called The Farm, even though there weren't any cows or chickens or anything. There was a field out back, though, and Bubbles would take me on walks through the tall, sweet-smelling grass. I would hide and she'd say loudly, "Oh no! Have I lost her again?" I'd wait until I felt like I might burst, then I'd spring up and surprise her. She would always explode with laughter and what seemed like genuine relief, and then she'd take my hand and walk me back to put the kettle on. Along the way, she'd find me some sort of treasure—part of a robin's egg, or a dragonfly wing, or a curly piece of silver tree bark— that would appear like magic.

For a long time, I believed Bubbles was part fairy.

She was beautiful, and her ratty old paint-splattered clothes only made her look even more so, like Cinderella before the ball. Bubbles tossed around Yiddish words, like Ace, but they were always nice ones like *kvell*, which means "to be proud of something or someone." Or she'd say *nem a shtikl*, which means "have a little piece of something." "Nem a shtikl, Zeldaleh," she'd say when our tea was ready, pushing a plate of cake toward me: honey cake or coffee cake, or my favorite, lemon.

But then Bubbles got sick. And it turned out she had cancer. She had it real bad, and it changed everything. At first, she wore scarves on her head, but her eyes still sparkled and she could still sit out behind The Farm and paint. But then she got so tired that even painting was too much, and my mom and dad started talking about moving to Vermont. The plan was that we'd go help her out while she got better.

But here's the thing: She didn't. Get better, that is. When she died, we flew to Vermont and stayed at The Farm for a week while Bubbles and Ace's friends and neighbors kept showing up with platters of cold cuts and pastries. The whole thing didn't feel real. I kept expecting Bubbles to appear at the door like she had with the giraffe card. "Surprise!" Flying back to New York and even going back to school felt like a huge relief. Until a few weeks later when I heard my dad on the phone, talking about how many boxes we'd need.

"What do we need boxes for?" I asked.

"Oh!" said my dad, looking surprised and maybe even a little guilty. "Well, remember how we were planning to spend some time in Vermont this spring?"

"Sure," I said. "But that was before Bubbles . . ." My voice trailed off.

"I know," said my dad. "Your mom and I have been talking about it, and we feel like we should go anyway."

"Go?" I asked.

"Go," repeated my dad. There was something about the way he said it. That plus the boxes.

"You mean *move?*" I asked.

My dad nodded.

"Permanently?"

"Well, we'll see," said my dad. "Maybe, if we like it there."

"I like it *here*," I told him. I had lived in Brooklyn my whole life. So had my dad, for that matter.

"Me too," he admitted. "But not to worry, Zelly. It's going to be an adventure." Which is the kind of thing he always says if he wants to get me to go to the grocery store with him when he knows perfectly well I'd rather stay home and watch TV.

"How do you figure?" I asked him.

My dad grinned. "Well, if living with Ace isn't an adventure, I don't know what is."

"We're moving to The Farm?" I asked.

"Not exactly," said my dad. He went on to explain that Ace was selling The Farm. My dad and mom had put an offer in on a house in Vermont and invited Ace to move in with

us. "Ace is all alone," explained my dad. "He really needs our help right now."

"Now? Like *now* now? But what about school?" I asked.

"Well, as luck would have it, they have schools there too," said my dad.

"Seriously, Dad," I said.

"I know this might sound kind of zany, Zellybean," said my dad, who likes to dust off my old baby nicknames whenever he gets a chance, "but I think this could be a good thing for all of us. And since Ace really needs us right now, this just makes more sense than running up and back all the time and making ourselves crazy."

"Why can't Ace just move back to Brooklyn?" I asked.

My dad gave me a look. "Have you ever tried to make Ace do something he didn't want to do?" he said.

So, just like that, the plan went from moving to Vermont for a little while to help Bubbles and Ace until Bubbles got better to moving there forever and having Ace move in with us. With no Bubbles. Which sounded to me like if the cafeteria at school was serving pizza with Brussels sprouts, but then when you got to the front of the line, they said, "Sorry. We're out of pizza." So all you got was the Brussels sprouts, a big, overflowing pile of them.

Bubbles was no Brussels sprout. And if she was pizza, she would have been the best pizza in the world. Bubbles always fussed over me. She'd grab my hands and cup hers around them, telling me "Your hands are so cold!" And calling me

shayna, which means "beautiful": "Come in, *shayna velt*, take your coat off," or "Give me a kiss, *shayna punim!*" And even though I know I'm not beautiful—with my bushy hair, my glasses, and my way-too-many freckles—when she called me "beautiful face," she made me feel that way. Bubbles is my biggest fan.

I mean *was*.

I always forget.

I looked over at Sam and Ace—Ace still bragging about catching fish and Sam hanging on his every word.

Ace is a pile of Brussels sprouts and then some.

And that was even before he came up with the whole "practice dog" business.

I didn't remember putting the Dumb Old Jug into the car, but when we got out at the orchard, there he was in the way back of our station wagon.

"Please don't tell me I have to drag the Dumb Old Jug around while we pick," I whispered to my mom as she hoisted our cooler out of the car.

"This is between you and your grandfather" came her whispered reply. Then, in her regular voice, she said, "Here, carry this." She handed me a shopping bag filled with empty Tupperware containers and lids.

"O.J.'s not allowed! O.J.'s not allowed!" chanted Sam in a singsong voice.

"What do you mean?" I asked, catching up with him. Sam

pointed to a big wooden sign next to the farm stand. The sign said:

OUR DOGS, JESSE AND ROXIE, ASK THAT ALL OTHER DOGS REMAIN AT HOME OR TIED TO THE HITCHING POST. SORRY, THEY'RE THE BOSSES!

I smiled. "Oh well," I said happily. O.J. would have to remain in the car.

Ace joined us and read the sign. "HMMMPH!" he said. "WELL, WHAT ARE YOU WAITING FOR? HITCH HIM UP."

"Grandpa, O.J. is fine in the car."

"YOU CAN'T LEAVE A DOG IN A CAR ON A HOT DAY!"

"Well, okay, we'll leave the windows down."

"NOPE. DOGS JUMP OUT. SIGN SAYS TO TIE HIM UP. SO, NU? YOU TIE HIM UP."

"Zelly," said my dad, picking up the cooler, "whatever you do, will you hurry, please? Your mother has informed me that cherry season is exactly one and a half minutes long, and I for one would not like to miss it."

"Oh, all right," I grumbled. I grabbed the Dumb Old Jug by the handle, trailing the leash. I walked over to the hitching post, tied the leash to it, and caught up with my dad.

"Happy?" I asked him.

"Look, Zellybelly," said my dad, "if you have a problem with this whole O.J. thing, you should talk to Ace. Don't drag the rest of us into it."

"Drag, ha-ha," I said.

"What?"

"That's what Ace said you do with a dog with no legs. You take him out for a drag."

My dad laughed. "You know, your grandfather can be pretty funny when he wants to be."

"He can be pretty annoying when he wants to be."

"That too," admitted my dad. "But you might want to cut him some slack, Zell. Remember, he's still grieving."

"Coulda fooled me," I said, thinking about Ace laughing with Sam and giving him noogies during the car ride.

"He is, Zell," my dad said quietly. "We all are."

As irritated as I was with Ace, it was hard to stay mad while cherry picking. The orchard was really beautiful, with trees that looked like pictures in a book. Bright red cherries were everywhere, shining like Bubbles had painted them onto the trees with her magic paintbrush. And many of them were doubles, which I hung over my ears and pretended were pierced earrings.

When I found the most perfect, brightest red cherry of all, I polished it on my shirt, then popped it in my mouth.

"Ewww!" I winced and spit it out. "Mom, these aren't ripe."

"Yes, they are," said my mom. "They're just sour cherries."

"Why are we picking sour cherries? Don't they have any sweet ones?"

My mom pointed to the next row, which had cherries so

dark they were almost black. "You can pick them too. The sour ones are for making pie."

"Oh," I said, and wandered over to the next tree. I picked a dark burgundy cherry and ate it. Mmmm, much better.

We stayed and picked until we had several full containers of both kinds of cherries. Then we lugged our cooler up a hill and ate sandwiches looking down at other people picking what was left of the cherries. My mom even packed some potato chips, which she never does.

After we ate, Sam and I climbed the trees at the top of the hill, and for once he didn't insist that we pretend we were in Batman's Bat Cave or something dumb like that. Down the hill from us, two big yellow Labs, which I guessed were Jesse and Roxie, ran around with a girl in pigtails. She threw a stick, and the dogs chased after it. Even though she didn't look like me, I could almost imagine that she was me and that Jesse and Roxie were my dogs.

My dad sat on the picnic blanket with his back against the tree, reading the newspaper with my mom curled up next to him. Ace sat in a folding beach chair, his lucky fishing hat tipped forward over his eyes, which meant he was probably asleep. Bubbles always said that one of Ace's great talents was that he could fall asleep anywhere. I pictured Bubbles sitting in a chair beside Ace and using her paints to capture the afternoon light filtering through the trees. Bubbles' paint set is like a smaller version of the box Ace uses for his fishing gear, but it has paint tubes and brushes packed inside it instead of hooks and lures. It's one of the only things of hers that I got to

keep, but I don't like to open it. Seeing all the colors that she'll never use again makes me sad.

Walking back down the hill, my mom and dad carried the cooler together, one at each end, walking side by side. Sam ran ahead, so I ended up dragging Ace's folding chair. I remembered how my dad had said that Ace was sad about Bubbles. I tried to think of some way to let Ace know that I missed Bubbles a lot too. But I didn't want to make him sadder. So instead, I said, "Today was fun."

In response, Ace announced, "DID I EVER TELL YOU ABOUT THE TIME IT SNOWED IN CHELM?"

Chelm? The made-up town that old Jewish people tell stories about? Chelm is supposed to be a village full of fools, or what Bubbles used to call "noodleheads," so all the stories involve the townspeople acting like idiots. What did that have to do with anything? And why was Ace talking about snow in July?

Without waiting for an answer, Ace started up, "IT WAS WINTER IN THE VILLAGE OF CHELM, AND EVERY NIGHT SNOW WOULD FALL AND BLANKET THE VILLAGE IN WHITENESS. EVERY MORNING, IT WAS THE SHAMMES'S JOB TO RUN AROUND THE TOWN, WAKING EVERYONE UP. BUT WHEN THE VILLAGERS GOT UP, THEY WERE DISAPPOINTED. 'THE SHAMMES MADE ALL THESE FOOTPRINTS,' THEY SAID. 'HE RUINED THE PERFECT SNOWFALL. . . .'"

As Ace rattled on, it dawned on me that I had never heard Ace tell a Chelm story before. The person who used to

tell me stories about Chelm was Bubbles. In fact, she some-times teased Ace by calling him "the wisest man in Chelm," which was sort of like calling him the king of the fools. I won-dered what Bubbles would have thought about Ace's Dumb Old Jug plan. I had a feeling she would have laughed out loud with her big thunderclap of laughter. I was so busy thinking about Bubbles that I suddenly noticed that Ace had finished his story. He stared at me expectantly.

"That's . . . funny," I said slowly, not wanting to admit I hadn't been listening.

Ace looked at me like I was from Chelm. "THEY PUT HIM ON A TABLE, SEE?" he repeated. "TO KEEP HIM FROM MAKING THE FOOTPRINTS. BUT MEAN-WHILE, IT TOOK FOUR PEOPLE TO CARRY HIM ON THE TABLE. FOUR PEOPLE? FOUR SETS OF FOOT-PRINTS?"

"Uh-huh," I said. "That's funny."

Ace shrugged. He seemed disappointed somehow. Maybe because I hadn't jumped up and down, like Sam would have. Or maybe talking about Chelm made him think about Bub-bles too. If that was the case, though, maybe it was okay to mention her. I decided to give it a shot. I said, "Bubbles would have liked it here."

Ace sort of snorted in response, but it sounded like he was agreeing with me. He looked down the hill at where my mom was now sitting on the cooler.

"IN ORDER TO BEGIN TO LIVE IN THE PRESENT, WE MUST FIRST REDEEM THE PAST, AND THAT

CAN ONLY BE DONE BY SUFFERING," he said, adding "CHEKHOV."

"Okay," I said, more confused than ever. I was pretty sure he meant his favorite playwright, not the guy from *Star Trek*. But with Ace, you could never be too sure.

Ace reached out one gnarled, spotted hand and put it on my shoulder. Our shadows bled together so they looked like one big, dark shambling thing with a lot of legs. Or maybe like a bunch of villagers carrying a guy on a table.

When we got to the bottom of the hill, my dad had gone to get the car, and Sam looked like he was about to fall out of a tree. I put down Ace's chair and joined my mom on the cooler. Ace immediately unfolded his chair, tipped down his hat, and fell asleep.

"It's nice seeing you spend some time with your grandfather," whispered my mom.

"I guess," I said, unconvinced.

"It is," she insisted, patting my knee. "Maybe this whole O.J. thing is a good idea after all."

"A good idea like you might actually say yes to a dog?" I whispered back.

"Zelly, do you ever think about anything but that?"

"No," I admitted.

"I didn't say that," warned my mom. But she sort of smiled while she said it.

Which gave me just the tiniest bit of hope. Maybe Ace, as weird as he was, was actually onto something. His O.J. plan

seemed terrible, but maybe it was the key to getting exactly what I wanted. Maybe Ace wasn't the wisest man in Chelm. Maybe he was just plain wise.

So when we got back to the car, I was actually relieved to see that the jug was right where we left it, tied to the hitching post. Only now there were two other dogs tied up next to him. Real dogs, not practice dogs.

"Good boy, O.J.," I whispered, trying the name out as I untied the leash. My mom was right—it did sound like a dog's name. Just then, one of the real dogs started sniffing O.J. I leaned over and picked O.J. up before the dog could lift his leg.

"Don't worry," I added. "I won't let anyone pee on you."

It wasn't until I got into the car and sat down with O.J. on my lap that I realized I had just started talking to an old orange juice jug.

Without a doubt, I was establishing myself as the wisest girl in Chelm.

When we got home, my mom and dad went to the kitchen to pit cherries, and Ace went to go watch golf on TV, which means take a nap. Sam went off to play LEGOs or something, and that left me. And O.J.

"Mom, can I borrow a permanent ink marker?" I asked. Because on the way home I had decided that Ace was right. If his crazy plan was going to work, I was going to have to convince myself that O.J. was like a real dog.

My mom fished one out of the junk drawer, and I took it, along with O.J., to my room.

Before taking the marker cap off, I studied O.J. His "body" was white, with a handle rising out of what I now decided was his "back" and some light green and orange markings on each of his two "sides" where labels had once been. That left his front, which was the side I saw when I turned the jug on its side, with the handle up.

I decided that the cap should be O.J.'s nose. With the pen, I carefully drew two eyes and a W-shaped mouth. I dotted in a couple of freckles for good measure on his cheeks. I turned the jug sideways and added a long, floppy ear, then turned it the other way and added another.

I turned the jug around again so the front faced me. A doggy face smiled back.

"Hi, O.J.," I said.

But something still seemed to be missing. Finally, I took the pen and drew a line all the way around O.J.'s neck, turning him to various angles to connect it. I colored the line in darker and made it thicker. Then, under his mouth, I drew a short loop coming down and a larger circle connected to it. Inside the larger circle I wrote "O.J." Now that he had a collar and tag, he seemed complete.

O.J. beamed up at me. If he had a tail, he would have wagged it.

Maybe Ace was right, I thought suddenly. *Maybe this plan is so crazy it just might actually work.*

If I had a tail, I probably would have wagged it too.

CHAPTER 4

"Zelly, time to set the table!"

"Coming!" I yelled, grabbing O.J. by the handle.

I set O.J. down under the table, then put out the place mats, plates, and silverware. When my mom left the room to tell Ace it was time to eat, I pulled out O.J. and quickly "fed" him. He smiled up at me the whole time. *Yum, yum,* he seemed to say. *Dog food! My favorite!* I slid him under my chair just in time. Everyone would see his face eventually, but there was no rush as far as I was concerned.

After dinner, we had cherry crisp à la mode, which was delicious. It was also shocking because we had stopped at Ben & Jerry's on the way back from the orchard. My mom is not a two-ice-creams-in-one-day kind of mom. But I wasn't going to say anything and neither was Sam. He picked up

his bowl and tipped it to lick the pink dribbly bits on the bottom.

"Gross," I told him. But when I saw that no one was going to stop him, I did the same. It was that yummy.

"So, any news on the Allie-gator front?" asked my dad brightly.

"Nope," I said, putting my bowl down. Once again, this had not been my lucky day in the mail department.

"Oh, sweetie," said my mom. "I'm sure she's busy."

"I guess," I said glumly.

"And she'll be home soon," added my dad.

"Can we please talk about something else?" I asked.

"Hey, you know what?" announced Sam, seeing his big chance. "One time, on hamburger day? Paul Harwood put a whole handful of ketchup packs on Andy Allen's chair? And then the lunch lady was like, *Sit down, young man!* and it was like *splort!* Only all over Paul!" Sam spread his fingers excitedly.

I rolled my eyes. "You and your friends are in a whole separate league of dumbness," I said.

"Zelly, that's enough. Apologize to your brother."

"Sorry," I said in my best robot voice.

"Zelly."

"What? I said sorry."

Meanwhile, Ace had apparently dropped something—probably his spoon—because his head had disappeared under the table. All of a sudden, he sat straight up, holding O.J. in the air triumphantly.

"NOW THAT'S MORE LIKE IT!" he crowed.

Everybody turned to look. And started to laugh. Sam laughed the loudest, happy to have an excuse to get me back. But my parents laughed too. I could see why: Ace was holding up an orange juice jug with a silly cartoon dog face drawn on it. But that didn't make it okay.

"Oh, right, *I'm* dumb!" yelled Sam. "You're pretending that's a dog and *I'm* dumb?"

"Give that to me," I demanded. Ace just stared at me, so I snatched the jug out of his hands.

"Zelda," said my dad sharply.

Instead of answering, I ran out the back door. As soon as it slammed, I sat down. And burst into tears. *What had I gotten myself into?* Sam was one thing, but what if he told his stupid friends? They were all babies like Sam, but lots of them had older brothers and sisters in my grade. What if word got out that I had a plastic jug that I pretended was a real dog? I used to be able to count on Allie to take my side, but now that she had gone to camp and become this camp person who didn't write me even a single letter, who knew? And what about the boys . . . ?

What if Nicky Benoit found out?

Nicky Benoit . . . I cringed at the thought. Nicky Benoit had been picking on me since my first five minutes at school in Vermont. My fifth-grade teacher, Mrs. Conroy, had met me in the hallway and asked me what I liked to be called. Then we went into the classroom together and she announced, "We have a new student. Please welcome Zelly Fried. She just

moved here from New York." And she wrote my name on the board in big block letters:

ZELLY FRIED

When she finished making the *D* at the end of my name, I heard a loud laugh from one of the boys in the back. But nobody said anything.

Until lunch.

I found a seat at a table with a bunch of girls from my class. All of a sudden, I heard someone behind me make a big, exaggerated sniffing sound. I turned in my seat and saw a boy—Nicky Benoit—standing there. He had dirty blond hair and dark, almost black eyes.

"P.U.!" he yelled, right in my face. "What stinks? Smelly FRIED egg! Ha-ha!" And then he started running around repeating it and holding his nose, and some of the other boys started laughing and saying it too.

I froze, startled. *Did I really smell bad?* I didn't think I did, though the last thing I was going to do was to try to check with everyone staring at me. Of course, I knew what his joke was. My family sometimes got wrong numbers that asked to speak to Mr. or Mrs. FRY-d, since our last name, which is pronounced FREE-d, is spelled F-R-I-E-D. But I'd never been called a *smelly* fried egg on account of my nickname being Zelly.

"Ignore him," advised the girl sitting next to me. She had long, straight blond hair all hanging down her back except

for one tiny braid by her ear. All around us were kids with shiny, straight blond or light brown hair. In Brooklyn, almost all of the kids in my class had dark hair. Thick, dark brown hair like mine; dark, shiny black hair; dark brown woven braids with beads at the end; or just plain dark brown hair. Looking around the lunchroom, I began to wonder if anyone in the entire state of Vermont had dark brown bushy hair like me. The lunch lady who grabbed Nicky and benched him for the rest of lunch had frizzy red hair, but that wasn't the same thing.

Another straight-haired girl nodded, her ponytail bobbing up and down. "He's a loser," she added.

I nodded too, trying to act like what had happened was no big deal. But inside I felt I might start crying, which I really didn't want to do. I couldn't believe this was happening. In Brooklyn, everyone knew how to pronounce my name. The principal at my old school had even been named Mrs. FRIEDRICKS. No one would have dared call her Mrs. FRY-dricks.

Quickly, I uncrumpled the top of my brown paper bag and peered down into it. There was an apple, some pretzels, and something square wrapped in waxed paper—strange, since my mother usually used foil—and several rubber bands. I pulled it out and unwrapped it suspiciously. Inside, I found a sandwich made of rye bread, mustard, and some sort of dark pink meat. I peeled back the top slice of bread and saw . . .

Oh no.

The girl who had called Nicky a loser looked at my

sandwich with interest. The girl next to her looked over too. She had a haircut I had begged my mom to let me get in third grade: bangs and one length all over. For the next six months I had to walk around with my head looking like a mushroom.

"Is that bologna?" asked the girl next to me, fiddling with her tiny braid.

"Uh, no," I answered without thinking, before realizing that there would be no way of explaining my lunch to them. *You see, I have this grandfather, named Ace. And he lives with us now because my grandma died. Well, he must have packed my lunch and he put in a tongue sandwich. Yeah, tongue, like in your mouth, only it's a cow's tongue. I used to like it when I was little, I mean, before I knew what it was, but now I don't, really. . . .*

For some reason, I suddenly pictured Ace standing in the cafeteria, defending the sandwich. "THE TONGUE'S WHERE ALL THE VITAMINS ARE!" he'd say. I imagined him opening his mouth wide and pointing inside while the straight-haired girls stared at his brown-spotted hands, his thick old-person tongue, and the hairs sprouting from all over him except the top of his head. "YOU PUT A SHMEER OF MUSTARD ON IT," he'd inform them, "AND IT'S THE PERFECT NOSH!"

I wadded up the sandwich as fast as I could and shoved it back into my bag.

"I mean, yeah, it's bologna," I lied. "I'm just not hungry."

I shuddered at the memory of that awful first day. Remembering the tongue sandwich made me think about Ace and his

ridiculous O.J. plan all over again. I looked down, and, sure enough, there was O.J., sitting on the back steps right next to me. I had taken him with me without even realizing I had done it.

He grinned his goofy grin at me. *"Time for my walk?"* he seemed to be asking. Ugh, three walks a day . . . That was going to get old fast. But as I stood up, the solution occurred to me. Ace had said three walks a day, but he didn't say where. As long as I stayed in our backyard, I could take care of O.J. without anyone finding out.

The leash was hanging up on the coat pegs in the back hall. Next to the plastic bags and a canvas bin full of Ace's precious rubber bands. After snatching these supplies, I set out with O.J. for a quick stroll along the inside of our fence. It worked like a charm! The fence was too high for people to see in. All I would have to do was slip out back three times a day and—

"FOR CRYING OUT LOUD! GIVE THAT DOG A REAL WALK."

A hand was extended out of the bathroom window and was waving what appeared to be the *New York Times Maga-zine* at me. Small problem. No one could see into our yard. But, unfortunately, someone could see *out* of our house.

"I . . . but . . . Grandpa, you didn't say anything about where," I stammered.

"VEY IZ MIR! I DIDN'T SAY DON'T WALK ON YOUR HANDS, BUT THAT SHOULD BE OBVIOUS TOO."

"Okay, okay. Fine!" I said with exasperation, stalking out

of the yard. A walk would do me good. It'd give me some space from Ace and a chance to clear my head and think. To figure out how I was going to pull this whole O.J. business off. Or, actually, to figure out *if* I was going to pull this whole O.J. business off. Hopefully, I'd figure out whatever I was going to figure out before I ran into someone I knew.

Like Nicky Benoit.

I dragged O.J. down to the corner. He made a little noise as we went, sort of a *skrit-skrit-thump* from sliding on the sidewalk and bumping across overgrown tree roots. Some of the trees in Vermont are huge, and their giant roots make the sidewalks look more like roller coasters than the flat ones we had in Brooklyn.

One of the nice things about moving to Vermont, my mom had been quick to point out when we moved, *is that you can walk around by yourself.* In Brooklyn, I was allowed to walk from my apartment to some of my friends' apartments on our block. And that was only if it didn't involve crossing streets and my mom could lean out the window and watch me the whole way. But in Vermont, I could walk down to the corner and turn left and be completely on my own awhile.

Another thing she liked to remind me of—*skrit-skrit-thump*—is that all the big trees keep it so it is never too hot in the summer. And, according to my dad, "When you blow your nose in Vermont, it blows clean."

"Vermont boogers are clean?" asked Sam the first time my dad made this observation.

"Well, what I mean is, there isn't any of that grimy junk like you get when you blow your nose in the City."

"What kind of grimy junk?" asked Sam, intrigued.

"Nate, what are you telling them?" asked my mom.

"Nothing," said my dad. "It's just, you kids should be glad we moved. Clean living. It's good here."

"I wanna hear more about grimy boogers!" whined Sam.

Dragging O.J.—*skrit-thump, skrit-thump-thump*—over the sidewalk bumps made by the giant trees' roots, I quickened my pace. O.J. sounded particularly loud, and I just wanted to get the walk over with. I turned the corner onto Summit Terrace, planning to go to the dead end. Allie and I always went to the dead-end part on our roller skates so we could practice our moves where no one could see us wipe out. It seemed like the perfect spot to take care of O.J.'s "business."

Just then, I noticed a kid I had never seen before sitting on the front steps of a white house with green shutters across the street. He had glasses and dark brown hair and wore a white polo shirt and shorts. His hair was wavy on top like you might draw the ocean, but it was short on the sides. He bounced a yellow tennis ball on the ground between his knees.

I pretended not to see him and stared at the houses on my side of the street as if they were suddenly fascinating. O.J. seemed to get louder all of a sudden. *SKRIT-SKRIT-THUMP, SKRIT-SKRIT-THUMP.*

"Hi!" the kid called out.

Oh no. I tried to walk even faster, as if I hadn't heard him—since I almost hadn't, thanks to O.J. But the next thing

I knew, the boy jumped off the steps and bounded down the street.

"Hey, um, hi. What's your name?" he asked.

There was no avoiding it. I stopped and turned, still holding O.J.'s leash.

"Zelly," I said.

"Sally?" he asked.

"*Zelly*," I corrected him. "As in Zelda."

"Oh, okay," he said. "Zelda what?"

"Fried. Why?"

"Aha! Jewish, right?" He smiled wide, and I could see the braces on his teeth.

"So?" I asked.

"So, me too!" he said. He tugged on his necklace and showed me the Star of David dangling from it, as if I had asked for proof. "I'm Jeremy Fagel. We just moved here."

"From where?"

"Brookline."

"Don't you mean BrookLYN?" I asked.

He grinned again. "Not Brooklyn. BrookLINE. It's in Massachusetts, just outside of Boston."

"Oh," I said, embarrassed. "Sorry. I used to live in Brooklyn."

"Brooklyn's great," said Jeremy quickly. "My dad actually grew up there."

"Oh yeah?" I said.

"What grade are you going into?"

"Sixth."

"Me too. Are you eleven?"

"I will be in October."

"Me too! October eighth."

"Yastrzemski," I said, out of habit. Everyone in Vermont seemed to think eight was a lucky number because it had been the uniform number of Carl Yastrzemski, the famous Red Sox player. He was such a big deal they retired the number eight, so now no one else can wear it.

"Yeah," he said proudly. "Hey, are you a Sox fan?"

"Not really. But the kids in my little brother's class went nuts when they found out his birthday is double Yastrzemski," I told him.

"August eighth?" he asked.

"Yup."

"What about you?"

"October fourth," I told him. I was already getting really excited for it, even though my family is a little too fond of practical presents. Every year, one of my gifts is a too-big sweater, and every year Ace says the exact same thing: "YOU SHOULD USE IT IN GOOD HEALTH." Whatever that means.

Just then, Jeremy said, "So, what's with the, uh, is that a milk jug?"

I had forgotten about O.J. "I, uh, that is . . . It's a science project," I lied.

"Cool!" said Jeremy. "Do you go to science camp?"

"No. I mean, it's actually more of a psychology experiment."

"Hey, my dad is a psychology professor!"

"Oh yeah?"

"Yeah! That's actually why we moved here. He got a job at the university, and it's tenure track, so my mom said we couldn't turn it down. Even though she hated the cold in Boston, and here it's supposed to be much worse."

"It's not that bad," I told him, though from what I remembered from visiting Bubbles and Ace at The Farm in winter, it totally is.

"So, what's the experiment?" asked Jeremy.

"Um, well, it was my grandfather's idea. He's a judge? I mean, he was, but he's retired from the bench." Jeremy nodded, looking super-fascinated. "He thought it would be interesting to see what would happen if I took an object, like this jug, and pretended it was a dog. To see how people might, um, react." Somehow, I had succeeded in making the reason I was walking O.J. sound even weirder than the actual reason I was walking O.J.

"Cool," said Jeremy. "So, are you trying to see if people think you are crazy and treat you differently as a result?"

"Um, yeah, I guess so."

"What are your findings so far?"

"I, uh, well, so far I just got started."

Jeremy frowned and nodded solemnly. "I thought you looked a little weird when I first saw you coming down the block. But not crazy. You should act crazier."

"I should *what*?"

"Act crazier. You know, to make people think you really believe you're walking a dog. Like, maybe petting it? Or playing with it? Like this." He got down on all fours next to O.J. and held up the tennis ball, which he had carried over with him, yelling, "Here, boy! You want the ball? You want it?" He bounced the ball on the sidewalk and caught it.

"Yeah, uh, maybe," I said, looking around to make sure no one had seen. I wished he'd get up.

"O.J.? His name is O.J.?" asked Jeremy, leaning in and squinting.

"No," I said.

"Then why's it on his collar?" asked Jeremy, pointing. He sat up on his heels and laughed. "Hey, I get it. That's funny. It's made from an old orange juice jug."

"No duh," I said. I was pretty sure he wasn't laughing at me, but I suddenly wished I hadn't told him anything.

"Jeremy?" A woman who also had dark brown wavy hair had come out of the house and was standing on the front porch. "Oh, there you are."

Jeremy picked himself up off the sidewalk. "Mom, check it out. This is Zelly. Zelly FRIED," he added meaningfully. "She's ten too."

"Almost eleven," I corrected him.

"Didn't I tell you? You were worried for nothing. Nice to meet you, Zelly." I could tell she was looking at O.J., but thankfully she didn't ask. "Jeremy, sweetie, I reached a good stopping point. If you want, we can go hit some balls now."

"Just a sec," Jeremy told her.

"Okay. See you soon, I hope, Zelly," Jeremy's mom said to me before she went back into the house.

"Do you play?" Jeremy asked me.

"Play?"

"Tennis." He pushed his glasses up on his nose and bounced the ball again.

"Uh, no." I didn't know how to tell him that kids around here play soccer, baseball, and hockey. Not tennis. And boys around here don't wear necklaces.

"If you want, I could teach you sometime. We can play for free at the university because my dad is going to be teaching there. They even have outdoor courts where you can play at night."

"Yeah, okay, maybe," I said.

"Cool!" said Jeremy, dashing toward his house. When he reached the other side of the street, he turned and yelled, "Bye, O.J.!"

I dragged O.J. down to the dead end, dumped him out, and cleaned up after him down there. It went a lot better than the first time, probably because I was pretty sure no one was watching me. Also, because there was less mess to clean up this time, and after the first disastrous mess I knew what not to do in terms of how to hold the plastic bag. After I disposed of the bag, I waited for as long as I could stand. I wanted to be sure to give Jeremy and his mom plenty of time to leave so I wouldn't run into them on the way back home.

When I finally got home, my mom was waiting at the door.

"Zelly, where have you been? I was getting worried."

"I took O.J. for a walk."

"To where? Brooklyn?" She gave me an anxious little smile.

"I'm sorry. I was talking to this kid. He just moved here."

"Really? Well, that's nice."

"I guess," I said. "He seems okay. It's just . . ."

"Just what?" she asked.

"Just nothing," I said. I added, "He seems like kind of a know-it-all." Which wasn't exactly true, but close enough.

"Maybe he was nervous," suggested my mom. "It isn't easy being the new kid. Surely you haven't forgotten already? It hasn't been *that* long."

"Yeah, I guess."

"Maybe you should give him more of a chance. It would be nice to have someone to hang out with."

"Allie will be back soon," I reminded her.

"I know," she said.

"If I had a dog, I'd have someone to hang out with."

"You have O.J."

"That's not what I mean."

Speaking of boys, now seemed as good a time as any to go deal with my brother.

"Hey, where's Sam?" I asked my mom.

"Dad just left to drop him off. He's sleeping over at Paul's."

Oh, great, I thought. By morning, every six-year-old boy within a five-mile radius—and all their brothers and sisters—would know about O.J. By tomorrow afternoon, I would likely be the laughingstock of the entire city of Burlington, possibly even the entire state of Vermont. *You know that girl Zelly? Zelly Fried? Get this! She has this old plastic jug? And she thinks it's a dog!*

By next week, the news would likely spread all the way to Camp Sonrise, where Allie would deny ever being friends, much less best friends, with me. By the time sixth grade started, there would be exactly one kid willing to be my friend: Jeremy Fagel.

Just then, I realized something. *Fagel* rhymes with *bagel*. Smelly Fried Egg, and her boyfriend, Germ-y Bagel.

Nicky Benoit was going to have a field day.

CHAPTER 5

The next day, when Sam got back from Paul's house, I was sitting on our front steps. Waiting for the mailman, as usual, but also waiting for him.

"How was the sleepover?" I asked.

"Awesome!" he answered. "We got to watch *Star Wars*. And Paul has these lightsabers, so I was—"

"Cool," I said. "Listen, you didn't say anything, did you?"

Sam looked confused. "Say anything? About what?"

"You know. About O.J."

"What about O.J.?"

I groaned.

"Sam, did you tell Paul about O.J.?"

"No."

"Promise?" It seemed like he was telling the truth, but I felt the need to make sure.

"Yeah, why?"

Okay. So far, so good. It actually hadn't occurred to him to say anything. But now that I had given him the idea, I had to make sure he wouldn't ever say anything.

"Because Grandpa wanted it to be a secret, okay?"

"Oh yeah?"

"Yeah, and if one of us tells anyone, he's going to be really mad and bad things are going to happen."

"Like what?"

Hmm, like what? "Well, you know how if Grandpa gets mad, his blood pressure goes up?"

"Yeah."

"And he could get really sick and everything if his blood pressure goes too high? Well, if you told and then that happened, you'd be in big, big trouble with Mom and Dad."

"What if you told?"

"Same thing, brainiac. That's why neither of us can say anything. So zip-o your lip-o."

Sam nodded solemnly and made a lip-zipping motion. Of course, since he often forgets to zip up his own pants, I can't exactly say that filled me with confidence.

With Sam taken care of and a lot of the kids in the neighborhood away, it was actually pretty easy to take care of O.J. without being noticed. I got in the habit of walking him early in the morning to avoid letting people see me dragging him

down the block. If Ace was napping or out of the house, I'd try to sneak a backyard walk. But then my mom set up stakes and chicken wire to turn our yard into a vegetable garden, so that was the end of that.

After a couple of weeks of walking O.J., something small yet monumental happened. I cut the *Dogs, Cats, Pets* column out of the newspaper and taped it to the fridge, like always. But for the first time ever, I came back later and discovered it was still there. No one had taken it down.

It's working, I realized, getting goose bumps at the thought. *Ace's crazy plan is actually working.* I grinned. *What kind of dog should I choose?* In my head, I began making a list of my favorites. A snuggly, smushy-faced pug? A whiskery Scottie? A beagle like Bridget, with long, velvety ears? Or a mixed breed . . . a snuggly, whiskery, velvety-eared one-of-a-kind dog?

Decisions, decisions.

Then, one morning, I came back inside after walking O.J., and I heard my parents talking with someone in our kitchen.

"Zelly," called my mom cheerfully, "guess who's here?"

Allie? I thought, even though she wasn't due back from camp yet. I ran in, and who should I see but . . .

Jeremy Fagel.

Sitting at the kitchen table with my mom, dad, and Sam.

"Thanks," he said, as my mom handed him a glass of orange juice. "I just figured out this was your house, so I stopped by to see if you wanted to volley with me."

"Volley?" I asked.

He held up a tennis-racket-shaped bag, which had been

sitting on the empty chair next to him. "There are some courts over at the university. We could just hit balls for an hour, if you want."

"Yeah, but I don't—" I started to say.

"I think I have an old racket you could use, Zelly," said my mom, jumping up. "Let me go look."

"It took me a couple of days to find you," announced Jeremy, looking pleased.

"Find me?"

"Yup. I saw you walk around the corner, so I was pretty sure you lived on Cliff Street, but I wasn't sure which house. I thought with the 'dog walking' I'd see you on the street again, but no such luck." He used his fingers to make quotes in the air when he said the words *dog walking*.

"How'd you track us down?" asked my dad, looking amused.

"I noticed your car because it has a Coney Island bumper sticker. But it also has a Red Sox bumper sticker, which threw me off at first because I knew you were from New York. But *then* I noticed that the Red Sox bumper sticker looked pretty new, so I figured maybe you got it when you moved because you knew how much people in New England hate the Yankees."

My dad grinned. "Nice detective work," he said. "Unfortunately, I'm going to have to kill you now."

Jeremy laughed. "Oh, I won't tell," he promised. "Besides, my dad is actually a Yankees fan too. He grew up in Flatbush. It drives him nuts that me and my brother Seth root for the Sox."

"I can imagine."

"But the truth is," admitted Jeremy, looking sheepish, "I still wouldn't have rung the bell if Zelly's shoes hadn't been out front. I recognized them from the day we met. Seth bet me I couldn't track you down, so ha! He owes me five bucks."

"Voilà!" cried my mother, returning to the kitchen holding up a tennis racket. "This was mine in college. Probably could stand to get restrung one of these days, but for today it should do okay."

Just then, Ace came into the kitchen.

"YOU GOT ANY TUMS?" he demanded.

Jeremy jumped to his feet.

"WE HAVE COMPANY?" boomed Ace.

"Hi, I'm Jeremy Fagel," said Jeremy, holding out his right hand to shake. Ace took it and shook it heartily.

"ABRAHAM DIAMOND, GOOD TO MEET YOU," said Ace, acting like Jeremy was some kind of bank president or something. "CALL ME ACE."

"Good to meet *you*, Judge Diamond. Zelda speaks very highly of you."

"IZZAT SO?" Ace looked over at me and raised one shaggy eyebrow like he found this difficult to believe.

"She told me all about the psychology experiment the two of you are running."

"THE WHA?"

"You know, the experiment. With O.J.?"

"You TOLD him?" yelled Sam, looking at Ace with panic and fear.

"It's okay. Grandpa said it was okay," I blurted, trying desperately to control the situation. "Right, Grandpa?"

"WHATEVER YOU SAY, KID," said Ace, winking at me.

"You kids better hit the courts before it gets too hot out there," said my mom, handing me the racket. I took it gratefully, happy to get out of talking about O.J. anymore.

"Can I leave O.J. here?" I asked.

"Has he been walked?" asked my dad, trying to keep a straight face. "We don't want any orange juice puddles on the floor."

"*Dad,*" I said.

"Sure, go ahead, honey," said my mom, giving my dad a *Behave!* look. "Have fun! Don't be too late."

Jeremy talked the whole way over to the courts. He did seem nervous, so maybe my mom was right about that. He told me about Boston, how he went to private school there and how he was thinking that public school here was probably going to be a lot different. Then he rattled off all of his favorite things. It turned out we both liked Greek myths and plain, not peanut, M&M's.

"And my favorite movies are Matt Malone spy movies," he told me.

"Yeah, a lot of the boys like those," I said.

"Wait, you've *never* seen one?" he asked, incredulous.

I shook my head. "I usually go to the movies with my best friend, Allie," I explained. "She's not big on action movies."

"Yeah, but these aren't just action movies. I mean, things

blow up, definitely, but there's a lot more to the story. He's a secret agent, so at the end, there's always a twist, you know? They're not just total popcorn movies."

I laughed. "As far as I'm concerned, popcorn is the best part of going to the movies." I told him about how Allie's mom actually buys us popcorn. My mom thinks movie popcorn is a rip-off. She always pops it on the stove at home, then brings it along in a greasy paper bag that she hides in her purse.

"No way! My mom too," said Jeremy.

He went on to tell me about Matt Malone movies in great detail. He was a huge fan, he said, and had seen all the other ones the minute they came out.

". . . and the new one comes out next month, and it's going to be awesome. I saw the preview back in Boston," he said.

"So, let me guess. You're going to camp out in front of the theater the night before it opens?" I asked.

"Yeah, something like that," he said. "But it won't be the same as seeing it with all my friends back in Brookline."

"Yeah," I had to admit. "Sorry."

Jeremy shrugged. "Whatever," he said. But he didn't look like *whatever*.

"I know how it feels," I told him. "I totally miss my best friend, Allie."

"I thought you said she lived here."

"She does. But she's at sleepaway camp."

"Oh. You didn't want to go with her?"

"Of course I did," I said. "But my parents said no."

"Bummer."

I nodded, and we walked in silence for a moment.

"So, hey," said Jeremy brightly, like he wanted to cheer me up, "how's it going with the psychology experiment?"

"Oh—that," I said, tempted to make something up. But Jeremy was being so friendly, it didn't feel right to keep pretending. I took a deep breath. "The thing is . . . Okay, don't get mad, but I'm not actually doing a psychology experiment."

"You're not?" Jeremy sounded disappointed.

"No."

"Then what *are* you doing?"

I cringed. "It's called a 'practice dog.' My grandfather came up with it. I really want a dog, but my parents said no. So my grandfather thinks if I take care of O.J., my parents will realize that I'm ready to get a real dog."

"Oh. Cool!"

I shook my head. "It's actually a really dumb idea. I have to walk O.J. two or three times a day and clean up after him." Jeremy looked confused. "Don't ask." I continued, "Which means any day now some kid from school is going to see me and tell everyone and the whole world will make fun of me for all eternity."

"Yeah, but, you know what? It sounds like it might actually work. And then you'll get a dog, which is what you really want, right? So who cares what some dumb kid says?"

"I guess," I said. But what I thought was: *I do.*

We arrived at the tennis courts. Three sides of the cage surrounding the courts were made of wire mesh with holes precisely the right size to catch and hold a tennis ball lobbed at them. The fourth side had a big green wooden wall with a white line drawn horizontally at about the level the net would be. Jeremy stood facing the wall with his feet apart and both hands on the racket, in what he called the "ready" position.

I tried to do the same. Then Jeremy moved over and bounced the ball, swinging his racket gently so the ball flew straight at the wall right above the line and bounced back toward me. *FWOK!* was the sound the ball made when it hit the racket.

My job was to let go of my racket with my left hand as the ball bounced once, then swing the racket back with my right hand and hit the ball toward the wall, aiming at a spot just above the line.

The first time, I closed my eyes as I swung, expecting to hear the *FWOK!* sound. When I opened my eyes, Jeremy was smiling, but he was nice enough not to laugh that I had missed the ball entirely. The next time, I kept my eyes open, but I missed again.

"Here, try this," suggested Jeremy, putting down his racket and bouncing the ball in front of me. I swung fiercely, determined to hit—

"Whoa! Watch it," yelled Jeremy, holding his upper arm. I had missed the ball and whacked him with my racket instead.

"Sorry!" I said, cringing with embarrassment.

"It's okay. I'll live. Try it again." He bounced the ball in front of me, then took a giant leap backward to get out of my way. This time my racket hit the ball, but it startled me so much I dropped the racket.

"I'm sorry. I'm hopeless."

"No, you're not. You should have seen me when I was learning to play. It just takes a while to get the hang of it. Try it again."

So I tried it again. And again, and again. Jeremy was really nice, even when I actually hit him with the racket for the second time. After a whole bunch of times, I finally heard FWOK! and I didn't drop the racket. Then I did it again, swinging with all my might. FWOK! I opened my eyes just in time to see the ball go sailing up in the air, flying high overhead to where it landed on the other side of the fence. I cringed, but Jeremy didn't say anything. He just bolted after it.

We played for a while longer, until I started to feel like I was going to melt. Even with all the trees, Vermont can still get pretty hot when you're running around a tennis court. Then Jeremy fished a handful of quarters out of his shorts pocket and bought us two Sprites from an old soda machine next to the courts.

"I should probably get back," I told him. Jeremy's glasses were slipping and his hair was extra-curly around his forehead, but he didn't seem anywhere near as exhausted as I was.

"Sure, you should probably check on your dog, right?"

"My dog?" I asked, before realizing. "Oh yeah, right. My 'dog.'"

"Why do you say it like that?"

"Because the whole thing feels like kind of a joke. I mean, seriously, do you actually think it might work?"

"Yeah, I do. And I'll tell you what. If it were me, I'd be thinking about upping the ante."

"About whating the auntie?"

"Upping the ante," Jeremy corrected me. "It means 'taking your game to the next level.'"

"Yeah, I know," I said quickly. I thought about how Sam always got things wrong, like thinking that the song lyric "The answer, my friends, is blowin' in the wind" was actually "The ants are my friends. . . ."

"It's sort of like developing a killer backhand in tennis so you can come out of nowhere and just annihilate the competition," he added, swinging his soda can like a racket and sloshing a little in the process.

"Uh, sure. Maybe next lesson," I said.

"Yeah, but I'm not talking about tennis. If I were you, instead of just walking O.J., I'd do other things to make my parents see that I was ready to have a real dog."

"Like what? Build him a doghouse?"

"No. Like *other* other things. For instance, do you know anyone who has a dog?"

I gave him a look of pure disbelief. On our block alone, there are six houses and seven dogs. "Jeremy, practically everyone in Vermont has a dog," I told him.

"Perfect," said Jeremy. "You can start a dog-walking service! I mean, you're walking O.J. anyway, right? If you add a

bunch of other dogs, your parents are bound to notice how dedicated you are."

"I guess," I said, considering the idea. It did sound like fun, getting pulled down the street by a whole pack of dogs on rainbow leashes like a big bunch of balloons.

"Oh, and, hey, is there an animal shelter here?"

"A shelter? I don't know. Why?"

"Well, if there is, maybe you could volunteer there. A friend of mine in Brookline had a birthday party where we all brought old towels and stuff to an animal shelter and they gave us a tour and said that kids could volunteer with their families. And if you got your parents to volunteer with you, they'd see all the dogs that need homes and, you know . . ."

"Right," I said, "and we'd end up taking ten or twelve dogs home."

Jeremy shrugged. "Just a thought. That is, if you actually want a dog."

"What's that supposed to mean?"

"I dunno. It's just how I do things. If I really want something, I try to figure out everything I can do to make it happen."

"Yeah? Well, does it work?"

Jeremy grinned knowingly.

"Have you seen my bike?" he asked.

CHAPTER 6

"Hey, guess what?" asked my dad over dinner. "I hear they have a first-rate Fourth of July parade here. And apparently, kids can ride in it if they decorate their bikes. How does that sound?"

"Aw-right!" yelled Sam, practically falling off his chair.

"Yeah, I dunno," I said. "I think I'll pass." If Allie had been around, it would've been a different story. We would've been all over it. We would have decorated our bikes together and pooled our money to buy enough candy to fill up our bike baskets. I pictured the two of us, riding side by side, tossing Starbursts and Dubble Bubble to the crowd. But without Allie, it wouldn't be the same. Especially since instead of candy in my bike basket, I'd have O.J. I remembered what Jeremy had said about his bike. Whatever he had done to

earn it couldn't have been anywhere near as difficult as taking care of O.J.

The next day, my mom tried to get me interested in riding in the parade, but I said no to her too. So she and Sam went to Rite Aid, and my mom let him pick out all sorts of decorations. My dad even carried Sam's bike into the house and up to his room so he could work on it there. Sam kept his door closed and draped a sheet over his bike at night so no one could see his project until it was completed.

On the morning of July Fourth, Sam called us to his room. He was wearing his Batman pajamas, and he looked tired.

"Sammy, how late were you up working on this?" asked my mom.

Sam ignored her. "Are you ready?" he asked. With a big yank, he pulled off the sheet. "Ta-da!" he yelled.

We all stared.

"Wow," said my dad.

Sam's bike, which had a black-and-yellow Batman decal on it to begin with, stood before us. It was decorated, all right. Decorated from handlebars to pedals to wheels in full-on Batman decor. We're talking black crepe paper, a huge black-and-yellow Bat-Signal on the front, more Batman stickers, and bright yellow and black pipe cleaners woven through the spokes.

Not a speck of red, white, or blue was visible on the whole bike.

"Sam?" asked my mom. "It's . . . beautiful. But what happened to the decorations we bought together?"

"They're over there," said Sam, gesturing toward his desk. Sure enough, on top of a pile of papers and a half-built LEGO Bat Cave was a large paper Rite Aid bag, the receipt still stapled to the folded-down top.

"Sam, it's a Fourth of July parade, not a superhero parade," I told him. "Batman doesn't have anything to do with the Fourth of July. You can't ride in the parade like that."

"You shut up!" shouted Sam.

"Mom!" I said, knowing how she feels about "shut up." But instead of telling Sam to apologize, my mom turned on me.

"Zelda! Don't talk to your brother that way. He worked very hard on this."

"Mom, come on. A Batman bike at a Fourth of July parade? Everybody's going to laugh at him."

"IN AMERICA, THERE IS FREEDOM OF CHOICE, BUT NOTHING TO CHOOSE FROM." This came from Ace, who had just entered the room. "USTINOV," he added. Ace liked to quote stuff.

"Do you like it, Grandpa?" asked Sam, looking genuinely confused.

Ace walked slowly around the bike, examining it as if it was for sale.

"I THINK IT IS SPECTACULAR," he finally said. Sam beamed, then stuck out his tongue at me.

"Impressive use of pipe cleaners," added my dad, who was on his knees inspecting Sam's weaving job.

"This whole family is nuts," I announced. But everyone was too busy admiring Sam's bike to hear me.

When it came time for the parade, I didn't want to go, but my mom made me. She said it wouldn't be fair to Sam if we weren't there to cheer him on.

"I could stay home alone," I suggested hopefully.

"Not up for discussion," said my mom, since she and my dad decided a while ago that staying home alone might be possible when I was in sixth grade, but not sooner.

"Okay," I said. "But O.J.'s staying home today."

My mom looked like she was going to say something, but I raised one hand. "Not up for discussion," I told her solemnly. "Marching bands make O.J. nervous. Plus he's afraid of balloons," I added.

So all of us—people, that is—went downtown for the parade. Pretty much everyone in Burlington was there, except for kids who were off at sleepaway camp like Allie. I kept an eye out for Allie's parents, though. Maybe she had sent a letter she wrote to me to them by mistake, and they'd brought it with them in case they ran into me.

It was one of those incredibly bright summer days that make grown-ups talk about the weather and the scenery even more than usual. I will never understand why grown-ups say some of the things they do. Ever since we moved here, my mom is always saying things like "Look at the lake!" and "Look at the mountains!" and "Is this a day or is this a *day*?" To be fair, Lake Champlain is a really nice lake, and the

Green Mountains and Camel's Hump are pretty too. But it's not like they change from day to day.

In the parade, the police came first, riding their motorcycles. Next came a Veterans of Foreign Wars float, and then some Morgan horses marched by with their manes and tails braided and their chestnut coats gleaming. The Burlington High School marching band played "Yankee Doodle Dandy," and the football team and cheerleaders threw Tootsie Rolls and these little laminated cards with the fall game schedule on them. The University of Vermont mascot, the Catamount, which looked sort of like a lion (but without the mane) or a tiger (but without the stripes), rode by in a dark green convertible.

"Isn't this great?" asked my mom, holding one hand over her eyes and craning her neck to see what was coming up next.

"It's okay," I told her. "Remember the Halloween parade in the City last year? There were those fifty-foot-tall marching puppets?"

"Do you know who made those puppets? Bread and Puppet Theater," said my mom. "They're from Vermont."

"Oh," I said. "Well, maybe they liked New York so much they moved there."

"Look, sweetie," said my mom, "this is a hard time for all of us." She glanced over at Ace. He was sitting in a folding chair next to us, ignoring the parade and working on the *New York Times* crossword puzzle. But the puzzle must have stayed

blank because people kept coming over to him to shake his hand or clap him on the back. "Ace! Happy Fourth!" "Another perfect parade day, eh, Ace?" "Morning, Judge!" Ace kept scrunching his caterpillar eyebrows and scowling up at the interrupters, even though he was clearly loving the attention. A waitress from Henry's Diner, Ace's favorite lunch spot, even brought his regular order out to the curb for him: black coffee and a scrambled egg on rye bread sandwich.

"I know you miss New York," my mom continued, "and I know you're missing Allie too."

"It's just that—" I started to say, but before I could tell her anything else, she interrupted me by yelling, "Dad? Get ready. I think I see them waaayyy back there."

Ace put down his *Times*, squinted at the marchers, and said, "I'LL ALERT THE PRESS."

I crossed my arms in frustration. No one cared a thing about me. All my family cared about was Sam, and they cared about him so much that they were willing to let him embarrass us in public in order to fulfill his dream of parading on his Batcycle.

"This is so embarrassing," I announced, even though no one seemed to be listening.

"YOU KNOW WHAT YOUR PROBLEM IS, KID?" asked Ace.

I didn't answer, knowing that in a matter of moments . . .

"NO CHUTZPAH!"

Ace would tell me anyway.

"What's that supposed to mean?" I asked him.

Ace grinned with satisfaction. Nothing made him happier than getting to talk about something he knew and you didn't. "IT'S LIKE MOXIE, KID. THE COURAGE OF YOUR CONVICTIONS. SEIZING THE REINS. CHUTZPAH!"

"I thought chutzpah was a bad thing," I said. Ace likes to yell, "YOU'VE GOT A LOT OF CHUTZPAH!" at people on the TV news.

"THERE'S TWO KINDS OF CHUTZPAH, KID," announced Ace. "I'M TALKING ABOUT THE OTHER KIND."

"Oh," I said. I suddenly remembered Ace saying something like this to me before. We had been visiting Bubbles and Ace in Vermont, back when they lived at The Farm, and they took us swimming at a pond. I didn't want to go in because the bottom was all mucky. Plus I had just read the Little House books for the first time, so I was thinking: *leeches*. Sam was splashing around in his water wings, and Ace had swum all the way out to a float in the middle of the pond and was gesturing for me to join them. I stood at the water's edge, shivering and shaking my head.

"COME ON, KID!" Ace yelled, commanding the attention of everybody in the water and onshore. "SHOW A LITTLE CHUTZPAH!"

But I didn't budge, so finally Ace gave sort of a wave that seemed to say *Forget about you*. And he dived back into the

water with a huge splash, and that was that. I still hate mucky bottoms, and I still don't see what chutzpah—either kind—has to do with anything.

Meanwhile, having issued the final word on the subject of me and my lack of chutzpah, Ace went back to doing the crossword puzzle and ignoring the parade. Case closed, once again.

"I'm going to go find a bathroom," I told my mom.

"Okay, but come right back," she replied. "The bikes should be coming soon. If for any reason we get separated, let's meet up in front of Ken's Pizza after the parade. Okay?"

I nodded, then wandered down Main Street. After I found a bathroom, I turned right on Church Street and looked at some jewelry at a vendor's stand across the street from City Hall. The prettiest earrings were pierced ones. Which is another thing I'm not allowed to do yet.

Just then, I heard a bark. Actually, a lot of barks.

I looked up and saw another table, but instead of earrings—*awwwwwwww!*—there were dogs. On, next to, and under that table were some of the cutest dogs I'd ever seen. There were two women sitting at the table, and one of them even had a tiny Chihuahua asleep in her lap. The sign hanging from the table explained it all:

NEED A BEST FRIEND? ADOPT TODAY!

I ran over to the table and dropped to my knees in front of an adorable fluffy brownish-tannish dog in a large metal cage. She had kind, sad eyes just like the dog I'd been doodling

since forever, the dog of my dreams. Immediately, her tail began to thump against the side of her cage. The pink card on her cage read: TALLULAH. 1 Y.O. KIDS OK, CATS OK. I offered her the back of my hand, and she licked it. Then I reached through the bars and scratched her ears. The dogs in the other cages—LOUIE, LILY, SADIE, CHESTER, GUS, DANNY, SOPHIE, and VEGAS—all wagged and whimpered, so I moved up and down the line, petting each and every one before returning to sweet, sad-eyed Tallulah.

"Aw, she likes you!" said the woman who didn't have a dog in her lap. She motioned to a stack of Chittenden County Humane Society brochures. "If you fill out the paperwork, she could be yours next week."

"Oh, I would love to. It's just—" I stopped, not wanting to admit that my parents didn't think I was responsible enough to get a dog. "I mean, I'd have to talk to my parents."

"Of course," she said agreeably, picking up a brochure and some other papers and holding them out to me. "Why don't you take an adoption form with you, and maybe you can bring your parents out for a visit to the shelter?"

Bring my parents to the shelter . . . Suddenly I remembered what Jeremy had said about upping the ante. "Actually, do you have any . . . I mean, do you ever let kids volunteer?"

The woman smiled broadly. "What a good question! It just so happens we have a wonderful volunteer program for families."

She unfolded the brochure and showed me. There were photographs of smiling kids and grown-ups holding cats and

walking dogs, plus the address of the shelter and information about its services. As she talked about the program, I was already picturing myself there. Me and my mom feeding a roomful of dogs and then noticing one tiny little puppy looking particularly sad and lonely. I could see my mom's heart melting along with mine as the puppy nuzzled in my arms and fell asleep. Maybe we'd even adopt Tallulah too, so she could be like a mama to the puppy.

Clutching the brochure and papers, I dashed back to where I had left my mom and Ace.

"Mom, guess what?"

"Zelly! Oh, I'm glad you made it back. You're just in time."

Just in time for what? I wondered. But within moments the answer became obvious.

Just in time for the procession of bikes to arrive.

Red-white-and-blue-decorated bikes, some with big American flags taped to the back of them, red-white-and-blue trikes, even red-white-and-blue-decorated wagons were everywhere. Kids wore red-white-and-blue overalls, sunglasses, bandannas, T-shirts, and shorts. One girl even wore a sparkly red-and-white bathing suit with a bright blue tutu. I saw Jeremy, but he was way on the other side of the pack, riding a shiny silver mountain bike and wearing a blue polo shirt, white tennis shorts, and his Red Sox baseball cap.

And then there was my brother.

In his black Batman costume.

Riding his black Batman bike.

For a second, I dared to hope that no one noticed him.

But some of the littlest kids were riding slow, and Jeremy and the others were riding fast, and Sam was somewhere in the middle. So the fast kids clumped together and moved ahead, and the slow kids clumped together and lagged behind.

And in the middle, riding all alone, was Batman.

My mom was clapping and cheering. My dad, who had been with Sam until the parade started, had joined her. He was clapping too, and taking pictures. But no one probably would have noticed them or connected them—and me—to the wacky Batman kid in the parade . . .

If it hadn't been for Ace.

As Sam got closer, Ace stood up. And in his booming, barrelly voice, he began to yell at the top of his lungs.

"THAT'S MY BOY! ATTABOY, SAMMY! ATTABOY!"

Suddenly it felt like everyone around us had stopped staring at the parade. Instead, they were staring at Ace, whose idea of patriotic attire was a bright yellow Katz's Delicatessen SEND A SALAMI TO YOUR BOY IN THE ARMY T-shirt and his lucky fishing hat, which has a pattern of Budweiser beer logos all over it.

And then I heard it.

It started quietly, but it got louder and louder as the crowd recognized and picked up the cheer. And loudest of all when Ace joined in:

> *Na-na-na-na*
> *Na-na-na-na*
> *Na-na-na-na*

Na-na-na-na
Batman!!!

At the sound of his theme song, Sam sat up taller, doing his best, most serious Batman face. It was his dream come true: He wasn't just Sam-being-Batman. He *was* Batman. He lifted one hand from the handlebars—his training wheels keeping him from tipping over—and waved to the crowd, which exploded into applause.

"Yeah, Batman!" "Go, Batman!" people called.

It was beyond embarrassing. It even made me wish I had ridden in the parade after all. I could have covered my bike with red, white, and blue decorations, just like the rest of the kids, and no one would have known that the weirdo kid in the Batman outfit—not to mention his weirdo grandfather—were related to me. I could've ridden fast, flying past Ace before he even looked up from his crossword puzzle and noticed me, and missed the whole Batman scene altogether. Instead, I was stuck right in the middle of it. Standing between my parents and Ace, I was obviously none other than Batman's big sister.

Across the street, I suddenly noticed Nicky Benoit. He was standing next to a much bigger kid—practically a grown-up—who had the same beady little eyes as Nicky. From the snarly mean smile on Nicky's face, I could tell he had something to say about me and my family.

"Hey, Smelly Fried Egg," he'd probably say the next chance he got. "I knew you were stinky, but I didn't know

your little brother was completely cracked. Ha-ha! Get it? Stinky Cracked Egg?"

And I stood there, frozen, wishing to be somewhere, anywhere else. In Brooklyn, maybe, or in that big field that used to be behind The Farm. Looking for treasures with Bubbles or just running with Tallulah and the puppy chasing after me. Wishing to be someone else too. Some other kid, part of some other family, one of those families who dressed normally and whose kids decorated their bikes normally and who would have said yes to Camp Sonrise. So instead of being here right now, I'd be far away, arm in arm with my best friend, singing songs or doing craft projects.

Maybe even making some fudge.

CHAPTER 7

After the parade, we went home, and I tried—hard—to put the whole Batman episode out of my mind. Which was made harder by the fact that Sam refused to take off his costume and kept running around singing his theme song. Luckily, distraction came in the form of our next-door neighbors, the Stanleys, who we had invited over for a cookout. Unfortunately, the best thing about the Stanleys is their beagle, Bridget, who it turned out they had left at home. From our backyard, we could hear her howling on the other side of the fence.

"Cool it, Bridget!" yelled Mr. Stanley in the direction of their house.

Mrs. Stanley shook her head, amused. "Bob!" she said. "You know she can't hear you."

"Can I go get her?" I asked Mrs. Stanley. I was pretty sure Bridget was making so much noise because she felt left out. It's true she can't see or hear that well anymore, but I'm pretty sure she still senses stuff somehow. Mrs. Stanley said it was okay with her, so I went around to their gate. Since I didn't have a leash and since she's so old, I carried Bridget to our yard. Bridget didn't seem to mind. In fact, she licked my face a lot to say thanks for getting her an invite to our party.

My dad was in a really good mood, tending the grill and wearing his red KISS THE COOK apron, which my mom gave him for his birthday last year. And the cookout got much better once Bridget was there. Her favorite thing is being scratched under her chin. When you do that, she loves it so much she kind of falls over and then demands what Mr. Stanley calls the Belly Treatment. Wait a second. Maybe taking care of Bridget could be part of upping the ante. I was just going to ask about this when Ace came out of the house. He was wearing an apron like my dad, only his apron was white and said I LOVE SHIKSAS on it.

"'I love shiksas,'" read Mrs. Stanley. "Is that like shiksa-bob?" she asked. I heard my dad almost choke on his Pepsi.

Ace gave her a kind of amused smile. "SURE," he said. "I LIKE YOU GUYS . . . SHIKSA AND BOB." He gestured to each of them, palms up.

"Ace," scolded my dad, "remember how you said you'd behave?"

"WHA?"

My dad turned to the Stanleys. "Ace is making a little joke. A *shiksa* means 'a non-Jewish woman.'"

"Oh!" said Mrs. Stanley. "I see."

"It's not a derogatory term," my dad told them. "At least, not in this context."

"Well, I learned something new today, didn't I?" said Mrs. Stanley, nodding at Ace. Ace shrugged.

"Dad, can I have a word with you? In the kitchen?" called my mom through the screen door.

Ace shrugged again, but he headed inside. Since Ace had moved in with us, my mom would periodically try to "have a word" with him. It usually ended with Ace storming off, yelling something like, "THIS LIVING ARRANGEMENT WAS YOUR BRIGHT IDEA, MARILYNN, NOT MINE."

Bridget came over to me and started butting me with her head, so I sat down on the grass next to her and began scratching her chin again. With a contented *wurfff!* Bridget flopped over on her back and presented her stomach. *Belly Treatment! Belly Treatment!* she practically begged. "Oh, all right," I told her teasingly.

"Mrs. Stanley?" I asked, scratching Bridget's stomach while she wriggled with pleasure. "I was wondering if you might need someone to walk Bridget sometimes?"

"Oh," said Mrs. Stanley, looking at Bridget, then looking over at Mr. Stanley. "Well, yes, sometimes. Although usually we just take her with us to our camp."

"Your . . . camp?" This didn't make any sense. Grown-ups didn't go to sleepaway camp.

My dad, who had been listening, laughed. "It's not a camp like you're thinking, Zelly. A *camp* is another name for a summer house."

"Oh," I said, feeling stupid.

Mrs. Stanley laughed too. "It's nothing fancy. Just a little cottage on the lake where we go on weekends and for a longer stay in August. A 'camp' is what everyone around here calls it. I always forget that you're not from here!"

She said it in a nice way, but my heart kind of fell anyway. Mrs. Stanley obviously hadn't seen Batman in action that morning. The parade had made it pretty clear to everyone in the Greater Burlington area that our family was definitely Not from Here.

"I'd just as soon leave her home when we go next weekend," chimed in Mr. Stanley. "If you want, you can take care of Bridget then. That is, if it's okay with Bridget. OKAY, BRIDGET?"

Bridget seemed to hear something, so she ran toward Mr. Stanley, crashing into the picnic table in the process.

I ran over and knelt down beside her.

"Heyyyy, Bridgie," I said. "You okay, old girl?"

Bridget gazed happily up at me with her milky eyes. Her tail began to wag. *Time for more Belly Treatment?* she seemed to say.

"Dad?" I asked later, after the Stanleys went home. "Did you hear I'm going to be taking care of Bridget?"

"I did," said my dad, spooning coleslaw from a bowl back into a plastic deli container.

"And do you remember how you said when we moved here that it wasn't a good time to get a dog?"

"Sounds like something I could have said, yes."

"Well, is now a better time?"

"A better time for what?"

"To get a dog?"

"Speaking of dogs," said my mom, carrying in a platter, "what shall I do with these extra ones that are cooked but didn't get eaten?"

"We should keep them. Ace will eat them," said my dad.

"Dad!" I said. "I'm trying to talk to you about something important."

"Oh. I'm sorry. Say it again."

"I said, can we get a dog? Can I get a dog?"

My dad sighed. "Zellyboo, haven't we been over this?"

"Well, yeah, but not since I got O.J. I'm almost eleven now too. Plus I'm going to be taking care of Bridget."

"Zelly, that's just for a couple of days. Owning a dog is for ten or fifteen years. That's a big commitment that I'm not sure your mother and I are ready to make."

"You guys wouldn't have to do anything! It would be my dog."

My dad raised an eyebrow. "Uh-huh," he said evenly.

"It would!"

"Every day? Every walk? Even if it is raining? Or snowing? If you think it snows a lot in Brooklyn, just wait till you see how much it snows here in Vermont."

"I know, Dad. Please!"

My dad put the coleslaw in the fridge, then went over to the sink and started using the spray hose to wash off a pan that had been soaking.

"So?" I said.

"So what?"

"So, can I get a dog?"

"Zelly, I just told you what I think. If you need an answer right now, the answer is no. And if you insist on discussing this any further," he paused and pointed the spray hose at me, "I shall be forced to use this."

"SPEAKING OF DOGS, YOU GOT ANY LEFT?" asked Ace, who had wandered into the kitchen. "I COULD USE A LITTLE NOSH."

My mom put the platter of cold grilled hot dogs on the kitchen table and said, "Dad, sit down. I'll get you a plate."

"Mom," I tried one last time, "can I talk to you in my room?"

"Sweetie, if this is about the dog thing, I agree with your dad. It is a big responsibility, so it is a decision we need to make as a family."

"What about if I start a dog-walking service? Or volunteer at an animal shelter, or both?"

"Those sound like great ideas."

"Really?" I asked.

"Sure! That way, even if we don't end up getting a dog, you'll still be able to spend as much time as you want with animals."

"They didn't go for it," I told Jeremy the next day on the way to the tennis courts.

"Who didn't go for what?"

"My parents didn't think dog walking or volunteering would make any difference. In fact, they think those are great ideas because they'll give me plenty of time with dogs without having to actually get a dog!"

"Wait, did you really *do* those things?"

"No. But, like I told you, it wouldn't matter."

Jeremy, who had been trying to balance his racket on one finger while walking, lunged forward to keep from dropping it. "It might," he told me.

"How do you figure?"

Jeremy caught his racket as it fell, then set it up on his finger again. "You can't just talk the talk. You have to show them. You have to actually do it."

"Okay, so . . . how?"

Jeremy's racket fell again. This time, he picked it up and put it back in his bag. "C'mon," he said. "I have an idea."

By the time we got back to my house, I was as hot and sweaty as if we had played tennis. Jeremy's idea had been to go by his dad's office, where we were able to use a computer and printer to make flyers for my new dog-walking service, The Zelly Treatment. According to the flyer, a responsible student (me!) would walk, feed, bathe, and groom dogs at reasonable rates, owner's (and dog's!) satisfaction guaranteed.

We printed fifty, borrowed a box of thumbtacks and a roll of masking tape, and ran around putting them in mailboxes and on every telephone pole and community bulletin board between the university and my house.

"What if I end up having to walk fifty dogs?" I asked Jeremy nervously when we posted the last flyer. I pictured myself, fifty leashes—fifty-one, counting O.J.—in one hand, getting dragged down the block.

"You won't," he said confidently. "But it's better to have too much business than too little, right?"

"I guess so," I said, going into my house ahead of him.

"There you are!" said my mom. "You two wouldn't happen to know anything about something called The Zelly Experience?"

"It's The Zelly *Treatment*," Jeremy corrected her.

My mom looked at us suspiciously. "Well, whatever it's called, it has two phone messages."

"See!" said Jeremy excitedly. "I told you!"

As I took the notes from my mom, the phone rang again.

"Yessss!" yelled Jeremy, pumping the air.

"Jeremy . . . ," I said, "I can't walk fifty dogs."

"Not even if it gets you a real dog of your own?" he asked.

"Uh, okay, maybe I can."

The Zelly Treatment ended up having exactly four canine customers, one of which was Bridget. I was also hired to walk the Dixons' German shepherd, Attila, who made me a little nervous because I had seen him wearing a muzzle before. Mrs.

Brownell said she'd pay me to give her poodles a bath, but they were so cute I offered to take them along on my group walks, free of charge. My parents, who were impressed with Jeremy's and my initiative, were less thrilled about the fact that we forgot to ask first, so they made us go take the signs down at that point. I was more than a little relieved, since taking care of four dogs—plus O.J.—seemed like plenty of work.

The only problem was, when I went to pick up the poodles—*grrrrrrr!!!*—Attila would start looking like he wanted to eat them, so I had to walk the small dogs on my left and Attila on my right, with my arms sticking straight out to the sides. However, the surprisingly good thing about walking a whole bunch of dogs was that O.J. wasn't so obvious. In fact, I could sort of loop his leash through my belt and he'd just lag behind, barely noticeable as anything but the straggler in my pack.

Unfortunately, O.J. still bounced around unpredictably and noisily, which sometimes upset the other dogs. Bridget would get confused and flop over to get her belly rubbed, and when she did, Maddy would take the opportunity to bark because Maddy barked at everything. And one time when O.J. bounced too close to Attila, he lunged forward with a growl, chomped onto O.J.'s handle, and shook him.

"Atti, drop!" I commanded, grabbing hold of O.J. to wrench him loose from Attila's giant jaws. Strings of drool trailed out behind him, connecting O.J.—and my hand holding him—to Attila's mouth like a long, wet leash.

"Ewwww!" I said, wiping my hands on my shorts. And my

shirt. And the grass. Attila licked his slobbery lips, clearly hungry for another taste of O.J.

The first couple of days of The Zelly Treatment went by in a blur, which was sort of good. Every time I checked the mail, my missing-Allie pangs would start, but then the dogs would distract me. And juggling my pack got easier when I didn't have to walk Attila anymore, and even more so when the Stanleys came back from their camp, although I was sorry to see Bridget go. Having her stay with us was almost like having my own dog, since she slept on my bed and everything. Although the truth was she slept so much it was a little like having a super-cuddly stuffed animal that needed to be walked.

When Mr. Stanley came to pick Bridget up, he pulled out his wallet and handed me two twenty-dollar bills. My eyes must have gotten big or something because he said, "It's okay, you earned it. Thanks for taking care of our little girl."

Still, I wasn't sure I should keep it. It was a lot of money, and I had only walked Bridget for two and a half days. Apparently, my mom agreed. "Forty dollars?" she said when I told her. "Zelly, you have to give Mr. Stanley his money back. They were only gone a day!"

"Two days, actually. Almost three."

"Still, that's much too much money."

"I know, okay? Besides, I wasn't doing it for the money. I love Bridget."

My mom smiled. "She's very sweet. I'm going to miss having her around."

"You are?!"

"Zelly, don't get any ideas," warned my mom.

"I'm not! It's just I really can't wait until I have my own dog."

My mom sighed. "I know," she said. I waited for her to go on, but she didn't.

"How much longer is this going to take?" I asked, trying to sound casual.

"How much longer is *what* going to take?"

I almost didn't want to say it, for fear of jinxing things. But she looked genuinely confused, so I said, real quiet, "O.J."

"What about O.J.?"

"Well, you know how I've been walking him, feeding him, cleaning up after him—everything? Plus walking all the other dogs too."

"Yes, I know."

"Well . . ."

"Zelly?" My mom looked concerned. "Did Ace promise that if you did all those things, something specific would happen?"

"Not . . . exactly."

"That's a relief. I was starting to get worried. Ace gets a little, well, carried away sometimes. You know what I mean?"

"Yes," I said.

"Good. Look, Zelly, I think your father and I have been pretty clear about this. We know you really, really want a dog

and we think it's great that you're practicing for it if that day comes. But that's not up to you. Or Ace, no matter what he's told you."

If that day comes, I thought. *Story of my life.* Somehow *that day* never seemed to come for me, even when anyone could see that it was time. Last fall, in New York, my friend Lena's mom let her get her ears pierced because Lena had to have one of her baby teeth pulled, even though she had said Lena would have to wait until she was eleven. If my mom said eleven, it would be eleven no matter what, even if I had to get *all* my baby teeth pulled.

Of course, when it comes to pierced ears, my mom doesn't say eleven. She says *twelve*. And when it comes to a dog, she doesn't even give me an age. I just get *if that day comes*.

Which sounds a whole lot like *never* to me.

CHAPTER 8

"So much for upping the ante," I told Jeremy.

We were on our bikes, riding over to the tennis courts. With all the dog walking, I hadn't seen him for days, so I had to catch him up on the whole O.J. situation, which seemed to be going nowhere faster than ever.

When we stopped at a traffic light, Jeremy suggested, "Maybe you need to add something else. Did you ever ask them about volunteering at the animal shelter?"

"Yes," I said. "But you have to do an orientation, so we haven't actually gone yet. Although I'm having second thoughts, since, if I go, I'm just going to want to adopt everything, and you know that's just never going to happen."

"That's what I thought too," said Jeremy pointedly. He chimed his bike bell for emphasis.

"How exactly did you earn that bike?"

Jeremy raised his eyebrows. "Trust me," he said. "It was harder than dragging O.J. around, that's for sure."

"Oh yeah? What did you do?"

The light turned green. Jeremy hopped on his bike and pushed off, calling, "Race you!"

"No fair!" I yelled, jumping on my bike and pedaling hard to catch up. We rode in silence, neck and neck, through the darkened campus, past the tall dorm buildings, gliding down the final hill to the tennis courts with Jeremy just barely keeping his lead.

I would've kept bugging him to tell me how he got his bike, but when we reached the courts, I forgot all about it. It was the first time we'd gone there to play at night, which took some convincing on both of our parts. My parents were worried about bike safety, which was why we both ended up with reflective tape on our shoes, racket bags, and helmets. And Jeremy's parents were also worried about other kinds of safety, which is why after some pleading my mom agreed to call and reassure them. And which is why we each had been loaned a cell phone to use in case of an emergency. Don't even get me started on what age they think I'll have to be to get my own phone.

Just as I had expected, it was really cool to be out on our own at night. The courts were lit from above by big lights, while everything around them was in shadow, dusky and still. The old soda machine didn't look quite so old because it was glowing, while the rest of the area was dark.

I walked out onto the court like I was stepping onstage

and struck a pose—ball in one hand, racket in the other—in the spotlight. The ball bounced up and down, its shadow stretching and shrinking dramatically. My racket swatted jerkily at the ball, fluttering through the intense brightness like the moths hovering around the lights. When it connected, the ball shot forward, and I stumbled back, excitement washing over me. And surprise, because I still hadn't figured out how to consistently swing with my eyes open.

Occasionally, the ball would set off toward the net, though more often it would arc skyward, like a shooting star. However, somewhere along the line, by practicing a few mornings here and there with Jeremy, I had gotten a little less awful at tennis. I had started to be able to swing the racket without missing the ball completely and sometimes even hit it at such an angle that it didn't go off in some crazy direction. When I did it right, the ball made this nice satisfying sound, sometimes *FWOK!* and sometimes louder, like *THONCK!*

We even got into a nice little back-and-forth thing there for a while, with Jeremy hitting it at the wall, then me returning it to the wall, then Jeremy, then me, then Jeremy, then—

"Hey! Hey, ZELLY!"

I turned, missing the ball entirely. The voice seemed to be coming from over by the soda machine, where three blobs stood in the shadows. The blobs moved away from the soda machine and toward the tennis courts. Jeremy looked over at me. I could tell he was thinking about the cell phones.

"Friends of yours?" he asked.

"I don't think so," I told him, even though I wasn't sure.

Just then, out of the shadows stepped Nicky Benoit, along with two other boys from my class, Jack DiPace and Devin Douglas, who were standing a little behind him. Nicky had something in his hand, which he was holding palm up, but I couldn't see what it was.

"Hey, Zelly, what's up?" Nicky asked.

"Nothing much," I said, trying to play it cool. I was glad Nicky wasn't calling me Smelly Fried Egg, but I knew there had to be a reason. Clearly, Nicky wanted something.

"Got any money?" he asked. Bingo. "I got pennies, but the stupid machine won't take them."

"No," I said truthfully, feeling a little relieved.

"How 'bout you?" Nicky demanded of Jeremy.

"Nope," said Jeremy. But he had one hand on his shorts pocket. It seemed pretty clear to me that he had brought some money with him. He usually did.

"Aw, c'mon," whined Nicky. "I'm thirsty. Are you telling me that *neither* of you has a lousy quarter?"

"That's right," I said, trying to sound firm and wishing he would just leave. I was glad he was on the other side of the wire cage.

"Aw, man!" complained Nicky. "C'mon, I'll pay you back."

"Sorry," I said, my heart pounding. Nicky muttered something and stalked back to the soda machine.

"You wanna . . . ," said Jeremy.

"Yeah," I agreed. I put the balls back into the can while

Jeremy zipped his racket into its carrying bag and slung it over one shoulder. PRINCE, the bag said on one side in big black letters. As we left the courts, Nicky was pounding on the side of the soda machine with his fists. Jack was kneeling down and sticking his arm up inside of it while Devin tried to rock the machine in place. None of it seemed to be working.

"STUPID PIECE OF—!" There was a crash as Nicky jumped up and karate-kicked the soda machine hard, making me jump and walk faster. We had just reached our bikes when—

"Hey, where are you going? Yoo-hoo, SMELLY FRIED EGG! Are you and your widdle PWINCE afwaid?"

"Just keep walking," I told Jeremy, knocking my kickstand out of the way and shoving my bike toward the road. Jeremy pushed his bike too, a little behind me.

"Oh, Pwincessssss!!!!"

"Why don't you leave her alone?" Oh no. Jeremy had stopped walking. He had turned and was yelling back. *Very* bad idea.

"Jeremy!" I whispered urgently. Nicky and the other boys had rounded the side of the tennis courts and were coming toward us.

"Oh my!" said Nicky in a fake high voice, charging forward. "The PWINCE is standing up for his pwincess." He switched back to his usual gruff voice. "Yo, Prince Charming! I've got something for you!"

Nicky raised his arm behind his head while the other two

boys laughed loudly, "Bwaah haa haa haa!" My heart began to pound, fast. Something awful was about to happen.

I didn't stop to find out what it was, though.

"Jeremy, come ON!" I yelled, hopping onto my bike seat and pedaling frantically. Hoping Jeremy was right behind me.

When I got to the dorms, I coasted to a stop under a streetlamp and tried to catch my breath. In a moment, Jeremy came into view.

"Are you okay?" he called.

"Yeah, I guess. You?"

"I'm fine," said Jeremy. He stopped, untucked his shirt, and shook the hem. He leaned over and ran his hands through his hair.

Ping, ping, ping. One by one, pebbles fell from his clothes and hair. *Wait, not pebbles*, I realized, looking at the ground. *Pennies.*

"What the—?!"

"I know," said Jeremy. *Ping* went one last penny. "Classic, right?"

"Classic?!" I said.

"Yeah. Bullies love to throw stuff. Pennies, balls, you know. Pudding, on occasion." He smiled feebly. "Seth says I'm a bully magnet."

"Jeremy, this isn't funny."

"Of course not! But what do you want me to do?"

"I dunno. We can't let him get away with that."

Jeremy studied me. "You can try to show bullies they don't

bother you, but you can't actually make them change. It's true," he added. "My dad does research on this stuff."

"Yeah, but . . . ," I said, tempted to argue back but not wanting to defend Nicky. Besides, maybe Jeremy was right. I thought of all the mean things I'd seen Nicky do. Nicky calling me names my first day at school. Nicky putting thumbtacks on Kristin Garrett's chair. Nicky scrambling to the top of the climbing structure with Kirk Bowman's watermelon Blow Pop and taking one long, cruel lick before chucking it onto the wood chips below. Nicky had spent a lot of time in the principal's office on account of his behavior. It didn't seem to make a whole lot of difference.

Jeremy got back on his bike and motioned for me to follow him. Slowly we retraced our route through the darkened campus. Our bike race on the same path seemed like it had taken place a century before.

At my house, I said goodbye to Jeremy and went to park my bike in my garage. When I came out, there was Jeremy, still standing with his bike.

"Just so you know, I'm not saying it's okay," said Jeremy quietly.

"I know," I told him. But before I could say anything else, Jeremy chimed his bike bell and zoomed away, racing down the block, the streetlight bouncing off the reflective tape on his sneakers.

CHAPTER 9

When I woke up the next day, I couldn't help wondering if I had dreamed the whole thing. My stomach felt jumpy, though. Maybe because I knew it was no dream. Telling my mom what had happened at the tennis courts crossed my mind, but I squashed the idea just as fast. She'd probably call Jeremy's parents—and Nicky's, for that matter—so not only would we be dead meat when school rolled around, we wouldn't be allowed outside the rest of the summer.

Besides, my stomach was probably nervous for another reason. Today was the day Allie was coming home, at long last. Before Allie had left, her mom had promised her that I could go with her and Allie's dad to pick her up at camp. But now, after three whole weeks and not a single letter, I wondered if she would even still recognize me, much less care if I was there.

I thought about taking O.J. out for his morning walk, but the night before had made me nervous about running into Nicky again. Plus my mom's last word on the subject had been clear: O.J. wasn't getting me one millimeter closer to having a real dog. So I just left O.J. in my room and didn't feed him breakfast or anything. I knew if I saw Ace, he'd ask, so I went out back and climbed the big dogwood tree and tried to read a book in it while checking my watch every three minutes. At ten-thirty, I gave up trying to be patient and left for Allie's house, even though it's only about a five-minute walk from mine.

Allie's mom, Mrs. Schmidt, didn't seem surprised to see me early. She gave me a big hug, even though she's not a particularly huggy person. I guess she was missing Julia and Allie. We all got in the car, and Allie's dad drove us to the camp. The road was bumpy, and I was glad I hadn't eaten because my stomach flip-flopped the whole way there.

But as soon as I saw Allie, I knew everything was going to be okay. Her nose and the tops of her cheeks were pink with sunburn, but otherwise she looked like the same old Allie. She ran right over, yelling, "Zelly!!! Ahhhhh!!!! I missed you so much!" and jumping on me. Then, before I could even say the same thing back to her, she was talking a mile a minute about all sorts of things: some Noah's Ark play she had been in, the candle-lighting ceremony on the last night of camp, the totally cute boy over there ("Don't look! Okay, now look!"), and a girl named Krystal Wilton, who seemed super-mean at first but turned out to be super-nice once you got to know her.

When Allie's parents finally left us alone to get her stuff out of her bunk, I couldn't hold back anymore. "How come you didn't write to me?" I asked, swatting Allie on the arm, play-mad.

"Ow!" said Allie, pretend-hurt. "How come *you* didn't write to *me*?"

I looked at her, startled. "I, uh, I don't know. You were the one who got to go to camp. I figured you'd write and I'd write back to you."

Allie rolled her eyes and flopped onto her bunk dramatically. "Ugh, they made us write to our parents, like, every single day," she said. "After all those 'Dear-Mom-and-Dad's,' I guess I was just kind of lettered out. I'm sorry!"

I pretended to sulk for about a second. Then I picked up Allie's stuffed mouse off the top of her trunk and swacked her with it. "Just don't do it again," I growled. "Or Mousie gets it."

"Mousie!" Allie grabbed Mousie back and hugged her protectively. "I won't," she promised. "Anyway, next summer I'm not going to camp without you, and that's all there is to it."

Allie must have hugged about a million kids before we finally got into the car, Julia on one side, me in the middle, and Allie on the other. Allie rolled her window all the way down, leaning out and yelling, "Bye! Bye!!!" to everyone we passed. "Bye, Allison!" they all called back to her.

"*Allison?*" I repeated as the car pulled out of the camp driveway and Allie finally settled into her seat.

She smiled shyly. "What do you think? It sounds more grown-up than 'Allie,' doesn't it?"

"I like 'Allie,'" I said. *Did "Zelly" seem babyish too?*

"You can still call me Allie, okay?"

"Well, not if you don't *like* it."

"Oh, and don't be mad, Zelly," Allie added. "But I don't have any fudge for you. We didn't make fudge once the whole entire time."

"Who said you were going to make fudge?" asked Julia.

"Zelly's grandpa," Allie told her.

"Where'd he get that idea?" scoffed Julia.

In the front seat, Allie's mom and dad laughed. "Maybe he went to a different camp," suggested Allie's mom. "I don't recall ever making fudge at camp."

I guess Ace doesn't know everything, I said to myself. Usually, that thought would make me happy, but this time it didn't. It reminded me of just how wrong Ace had been about the whole O.J. business.

"Lanyards, yes," said Mr. Schmidt. "I made a lot of lanyards in my day. Some called me the king of lanyards."

"Look, Dad," said Allie, pulling out a long pink-and-yellow braided plastic chain.

"That's my girl!" said her dad, smiling in the rearview mirror.

"It's for you," Allie said, handing the chain to me.

I smiled and lifted my hair out of the way so she could tie it around my neck. I couldn't help thinking to myself, *This is way better than fudge*.

When we got home, Allie came over to my house and we went straight up to my room.

"What's that?" asked Allie, pointing at my bed.

I looked and there was O.J., sitting smack in the middle of my rainbow comforter, a note rubber-banded to his neck, completely covering his face. It said:

I'M HUNGRY AND I NEED A WALK.

I groaned and tossed O.J., note and all, off the bed.

"It's nothing. You know how I've been begging my parents to let me get a dog? Well, my grandpa had this crazy idea about what I could do to convince them."

I stretched out on the bed where O.J. had been, and Allie sat down cross-legged next to me. She giggled. "Did I tell you about the dogs? At camp?" I shook my head. "Well, we were rehearsing for the play and there were these two boys who were supposed to be playing the dogs? You know, on the ark?"

I listened for a while, but to be honest, it was kind of hard. After going to camp to pick up Allie—I mean *Allison*—and having to watch her with all her new camp friends, I was ready for camp to be over and our summer together to finally begin. After waiting as long as I could so as not to seem rude, I said, "Allie? Can we please talk about something other than camp?"

"Sure," said Allie, looking startled. "I'm sorry."

"No, I'm sorry," I said quickly. "I mean, I just . . . It sounds fun and everything. . . ."

"No, Zelly, that's okay. What's up with you?"

"Not a lot," I admitted. "I've been, uh, playing tennis, I guess."

"Tennis? Like at a tennis camp?"

"No. Just, you know, playing."

"With who?"

"Nobody. Just this kid who moved here. From Brookline. His name's Jeremy."

"Did you know him there?"

"That's BrookLYN," I informed her. "He moved here from BrookLINE. It's in Massachusetts."

"Is he cute?" she asked.

"No!"

"Tennis players are cute."

"Yeah, well, Jeremy's *not* cute. I mean, he's not disgusting-looking. He's just regular."

"Why? What does he look like?" asked Allie.

"I dunno. He's got glasses."

"Uh-huh. What color hair?"

"Dark brown."

"So, he looks like you?"

"No," I said.

Allie covered her mouth with one hand and pointed at me with the other. "You're blushing!"

"I am not!"

"Are too!"

"Can we please talk about something other than boys . . . or camp . . . for five minutes?" I asked.

"Yes!" she said, but I could tell she didn't want to. Still, to prove it, she said, "Do you want to sleep over tomorrow night?"

"Are you kidding? Of course!"

"Great. I mean, let me know if you can, because if you can't, I might ask someone else."

"What do you mean, you might ask someone else?"

"It's just that my mom said I can have three girls sleep over, and I definitely want to have you. But if you can't come, I might ask someone else."

"Someone from camp?"

"Maybe. What's the big deal? You're still my best friend."

"You sure?"

"*Yes,*" insisted Allie.

But I wasn't so sure.

Just then, there was a knock on my door.

"Come in," I said.

"Hi, Allie. Welcome home!" said my mom.

"Thanks, Mrs. Fried," said Allie, whose parents don't let her call other people's parents by their first names, even if they say it's okay like my parents do.

"Zelly, Jeremy called while you were out."

"Okay," I said. Allie gave me a look that said *Jer-e-my.*

"Also, have you taken care of O.J. yet today?"

I rolled my eyes. "No," I said.

"Who's O.J.?" asked Allie.

"I thought I'd do it later," I told my mom.

"Is Ace okay with that?" asked my mom.

"I don't know," I admitted.

"Who's O.J.?" Allie asked again.

"Zelly, I suggest you keep up your end of the deal," said my mom.

"Why?" I argued. "You said yourself it wasn't going to make any difference."

"That's not what I said," replied my mom.

"Yes, it is."

"No, I specifically said this was good practice for when you get a dog. I believe I also said if you make a promise, you should keep it."

"It's okay, Mrs. Fried," said Allie, jumping off my bed. "I'll help Zelly do it." She gave me a look that said, *Do what she says if you want her to say yes to the sleepover.*

She didn't have to convince me. I had heard the magic word: good practice for *when* you get a dog. *When,* not *if!*

"Okay, fine," I said. "Fine, I'll do it right now."

"Good," said my mom, leaving the room.

"Okay, now for the last time," said Allie, putting her hands on her hips, "what is the big, fat, juicy secret? Who is O.J.?"

"Oh, it's juice-y all right," I told her. I picked O.J. up and pulled off the note to reveal his face. "Allie, meet O.J.," I said.

Allie stared at O.J. Then at me.

"You have *got* to be kidding me," she finally said.

CHAPTER 10

"I can't believe your grandpa is making you do this," Allie said as we left the house to take O.J. for a walk. She kept just slightly behind me, looking over her shoulder nervously to make sure no one could see us.

"Believe it," I said flatly. We turned onto Summit Terrace while O.J. bounced gracelessly behind. As usual, I was going to wait until we got to the dead end to take care of O.J.'s "business."

"I still don't get why."

So I launched into the story of how Ace came up with the idea of me having a "practice dog" and how I signed on without knowing what it would entail. I told her about all the bad parts: feeding the "practice dog," dragging it on "practice

dog" walks, and, worst of all, cleaning up its "practice dog" poop.

Allie made a face at the last part. "Seriously?" she asked.

"Seriously. And once I even stepped in it!"

"Ewwww!" she shrieked. "Zelly, your grandpa is nuts!"

"I know," I agreed, even though I had a pang of guilt. And another pang of not liking her talking about Ace that way. It was okay for me to call him crazy or call his ideas stupid, be- cause he was my grandpa. But it didn't feel right for someone else to do it.

"Oh no," Allie said, freezing. "Quick, let's go back. There's someone coming."

I looked and saw Jeremy walking down his front steps.

"Relax," I told her. "That's just Jeremy. He knows about O.J."

"Oh," she said, looking over her shoulder once more.

Jeremy waved big at the sight of us and came bounding over, carrying his tennis racket.

"Hey, where were you this morning?" he asked.

"Oh no, did you go to the courts? I'm sorry! I thought I told you I was going along to pick up Allie at camp. This is Allie. Allie, this is Jeremy."

"Hi," said Jeremy.

"He just moved here," I added, because I didn't want Jeremy to know I'd been talking about him.

"Hi," said Allie, doing this little hair-twirling thing she sometimes does around boys.

"It's okay," said Jeremy, turning back to me. "I thought you meant next Friday. But it's no big deal. I just practiced my backhand against the wall." He dribbled a ball on the ground with his racket but ended up missing the ball and having to chase it down the sidewalk.

"Oops!" he said, laughing with his mouth open wide. "Do you play?" he asked Allie.

"Nuh-uh," said Allie, shaking her head.

Jeremy pushed his glasses up his nose and looked serious again. "Yeah, well, I can't play tomorrow morning because my mom wants us to go check out some synagogue in South Burlington."

"That's okay," I said. "Maybe we can play the next day."

"Yeah, okay," said Jeremy happily.

Just then, an older boy, who I figured had to be Jeremy's brother Seth, stuck his head out their front door.

"Yo, Germ," he yelled. "Mom says she needs to ask you something."

"I'll be there in a minute."

"Hey, is that the pooch?" called Seth.

"You told him?" I asked Jeremy.

"No, honest," promised Jeremy. "I just told my mom, back when I thought it was a psychology experiment, and he must have overheard. Just ignore him."

"Germ-y, NOW!" yelled Seth.

"I said, in a minute."

"Oh, so you want me to come out there and GET you?"

"Okay, fine! I'll be right there!" Then, dropping his voice to a whisper, he added, "Listen, I want to apologize for last night."

"For what? It wasn't your fault."

"No, I mean, for lecturing you." He looked embarrassed. "I get a little carried away sometimes."

Just like Ace, I thought. "It's really okay," I said.

"Plus it was my idea to play at night."

"Yeah, well, it could've happened anytime. He's a jerk 24-7."

"We should go," said Allie. "Later," she said to Jeremy, hooking her arm in mine and pulling me away.

"Bye," called Jeremy. "Nice to meet you, Allie."

We headed off toward the dead end. This time, Allie walked faster than me, and I had to really march to keep up. O.J. bounced gracelessly against the uneven sidewalk, *SKRIT-BOMP, SKRIT-BOMP*.

"What was that all about?" asked Allie.

"You're not going to believe this," I said.

"Believe what?"

And I told her all about what had happened at the tennis courts the night before. Allie's eyes got really wide when I told her about Jeremy standing up to Nicky and then Nicky throwing pennies at him.

"Wow," she said. "He must really like you."

"What are you talking about?"

"You're kidding, right? Jeremy! He's like a puppy dog for you."

Puppy? Oops. We'd made it down to the dead end, but I had almost forgotten about O.J. I looked around to make sure no one was watching, then spread out a bag and let O.J. do his business on it. Then I gathered it up, knotted it, and tossed it in a garbage can. I had become a pro at this. Allie shook her head, watching me.

"I can't believe you're doing this," she said.

"What else am I supposed to do?"

"I don't know. Quit, I guess. I mean, you don't think this is actually going to work, do you?"

I sighed. "No," I said. "Although Jeremy thinks it could."

I was about to tell Allie what Jeremy had said about up-ping the ante when Allie said, "See! You can't stop talking about him! You *do* like him. Just admit it."

"Shut up! I do not," I told her.

"Zelly and Jeremy, sitting in a tree. K-I-S-S-I-N-G!"

"Shut UP!"

I turned and began to stride back toward my house, drag-ging O.J. behind me.

"Zelly! Zelly, wait."

I ignored her.

"Zelly, please! I was kidding. Come on, I'm sorry!"

I turned around.

"Take it back," I demanded.

"I take it back," she said.

"The whole thing."

"The whole thing," she agreed, nodding.

"Okay," I said finally. "But no more teasing about Jeremy.

I *don't* like him. I mean, whatever, he's okay, but I don't *like him* like him."

"Okay, okay, I believe you," said Allie. "Now, his brother, on the other hand . . ."

"What about his brother?"

"Don't you think he looks a little like Chaz Parker?" she asked hopefully. Chaz Parker played the older brother on the TV show *The Brothers Sleuth*. He was one of Allie's favorite celebrities.

"Uh, no," I told her. "I think Seth looks like one of those baboons with the blue butts you see at the zoo."

"Harsh," said Allie.

"And speaking of the zoo," I continued, "I think Nicky Benoit looks like one of those naked mole rats."

"Yes!" said Allie, laughing. "But with beadier eyes and uglier teeth."

We both wrapped our top teeth over our lower lips and did Naked Mole Rat Nicky imitations the whole way home. O.J. bounced along behind us, happy as always to be included.

CHAPTER 11

"I've got it!" I yelled, flying down the stairs to answer the phone. Allie had just left, so when the phone rang five minutes later, I knew she was probably calling with something she had forgotten to tell me. It was so good to have Allie home from camp!

"Hellooooo?" I said.

"Zelly?"

"Oh. Hey, Jeremy."

"I hope it's okay to call right now. My mom said your family might be in the middle of dinner."

"It's okay. What's up?"

"I wanted to see if you could volley a little earlier than usual on Sunday. My mom wants me to meet with a new clarinet teacher at ten."

"Yeah, sure, I— Oh, wait." I suddenly remembered that I was planning to sleep over at Allie's house on Saturday night. "Actually, I can't play Sunday morning after all."

"Oh . . . okay."

"I'm sorry. I just totally forgot that I'm going to a sleepover tomorrow night." *And usually the morning after a sleepover is the best part,* I thought to myself. There's almost always a yummy late breakfast and lots of talking and joking about the night before. I pictured Allie and me sitting at the table in her kitchen, her mom passing us a tall stack of pancakes and a pitcher of orange ju—

Oh no.

O.J. I had totally forgotten about him. Allie had said she was inviting two other girls. There was no way I was going to try to explain O.J. to them. But I couldn't leave him at home, or else I'd be in big trouble with Ace. And my parents, for that matter. That *when* would turn back to an *if* in a heartbeat.

"Yeah, sure. No problem," said Jeremy. "I guess I'll just see you a—"

"Actually," I interrupted, "can I ask you a favor?"

"Sure, what's up?"

"Is there any chance you can watch O.J. for me?"

Jeremy was silent for a minute. "I guess," he answered.

"Really? Wow, thanks!"

"Sure, what are friends for?"

I felt a rush of happiness. Everything was going to work out great. I'd show my parents that I could stick with Ace's

plan no matter what. I'd get to go to Allie's sleepover. And best of all, no one else would have to find out about O.J.

"When do you need me to do it?" asked Jeremy.

"Saturday night to Sunday morning," I said.

"Wait a second," said Jeremy. "Why aren't you bringing O.J. with you?"

"Um, one of the other girls is allergic to orange juice?" I joked.

"Or . . . ," said Jeremy.

"Or what?"

"*Or* you're embarrassed about the plan you made with your grandfather. You want me to watch O.J. so no one at the sleepover teases you about it."

"Yeah. So?" I asked. It seemed reasonable to me.

"So, I don't want to be a part of that."

"Don't want to be a part of *what*?"

"It's like lying to your grandpa," said Jeremy.

"No, it's not! Plus my grandpa doesn't care who walks O.J.!"

"Oh, really? Did he say so?"

"Jeremy!" I was getting really frustrated. "It doesn't matter!"

"Well, if it doesn't matter, why don't you just bring him along? Or tell your grandpa you're leaving him home."

"Fine, you want me to say it? I don't want people to make fun of me! Or tease me, or call me names, or throw pennies and pudding at me! Okay? Maybe you're okay with that, but I'm not!"

"Who says I'm okay with that?" asked Jeremy.

"You did!" I could hear my voice getting louder as I got more frustrated with Jeremy. "'Just let them know they don't bother you,' isn't that what you said?"

I suddenly wondered if the rest of my family was listening. The house seemed very still all of a sudden. And there was silence on Jeremy's end as well. Then he said quietly, "That doesn't mean I like it."

"Okay. So?"

"So, what?"

"So, are you going to help me or what?"

"No," said Jeremy. "I'm sorry. It just wouldn't be right."

"Great," I said. "Thanks a lot."

"Look, if they're really your friends, they won't make fun of you!"

"Like you would know anything about that," I snapped before hanging up on him.

CHAPTER 12

When I didn't come down for dinner that night, I was surprised to hear a knock at my door. I was more surprised to open it and find my mom standing there with a tray. She even carried up one of these folding TV tables we have that we only take out when the World Series is on or the ball is dropping on New Year's Eve.

"I brought O.J.'s dinner too," she told me, setting up the table next to my bed. And, sure enough, there was a small bowl of dry dog food on the tray next to my plate of spaghetti and salad and my glass of milk.

"Thanks," I told her.

She was halfway out the door when I said, "Mom?"

"Hmm?"

"Is there any chance I can leave O.J. here tomorrow night when I sleep over at Allie's?"

"Is that what you and Jeremy were arguing about?"

"Maybe."

"*Maybe,*" she suggested, "you could see if Ace would watch him?"

"Mommm . . ."

"Zelly, you want to know what I think about all this?" asked my mom. Before I could answer, she repeated one of her favorite sayings: "If life gives you lemons, make lemonade."

"What's that supposed to mean?" I asked.

"Well, it means to take what might seem like a challenging situation—"

"Mom, I know," I interrupted. "But what does that have to do with this? *Life* didn't 'give me lemons.' *Ace* did. And unlike lemons-into-lemonade, an old plastic jug can't be turned into something wonderful, like a real dog. No matter what Ace says. You said so yourself."

My mom was quiet for a moment. "Maybe not," she said. "But think about it. If it hadn't been for Ace giving you O.J., you might have moped around the house the whole time Allie was away. You never would have walked down past the corner and met Jeremy."

"Yeah, maybe," I admitted. Although it kind of seemed like we might not still be friends anymore.

"And if you hadn't learned to play tennis from Jeremy, you never would've become the Venus Williams of Vermont."

"Jeremy thinks I should just do what Ace says and drag

O.J. wherever I have to, no matter who laughs or how long it takes, until you guys agree to get me a dog."

My mom smiled. "And what do you think?"

"I think Jeremy's even crazier than Ace."

"Zelly," my mom said lightly, "why don't you tell Ace how you feel about all this? I know how he can be sometimes, *believe me*. But I still think it might help if he knew how you feel."

I looked at her. "Was Ace . . . always like this?" I asked. "I mean, when you were growing up?"

My mom did a perfect eye roll, which she must have learned from me. "Can you imagine Ace any other way?"

"But . . . how could you take it? He's so bossy and he thinks he knows everything and he doesn't listen to anyone and—"

"I'll let you in on a little secret, Zelly. You know who ran the show in my house, growing up? You know who was the real boss?"

I shook my head.

"Your grandma."

"Bubbles?" I looked at her, confused. "But Bubbles never bossed anyone around."

"And Ace adored her and would do anything for her. Just like he adores you."

I snorted. "Ace doesn't adore me."

"That's where you're wrong, Zelly. Ace is crazy about you. He just has a funny way of showing it."

"I'll say."

"I'm not saying he's not a pain in the tuchus sometimes," she said, getting up and patting her own bottom for emphasis. "But trust me. His heart is in the right place."

"If you say so," I said.

"I know so," said my mom.

CHAPTER 13

I thought a lot about what my mom said that night. When I got up the next day, I decided that maybe she was right. Maybe Ace needed to hear how I felt about the plan and how it was affecting me. So I took O.J. with me to go have a heart-to-heart talk with Ace.

I knocked on Ace's door. GONE FISHING, said the sign. *More like* GONE TO SLEEP WATCHING TV, I thought. I put my ear against the door and listened. Sure enough, I could hear voices and dramatic music.

I knocked louder.

"Grandpa," I called through the door. "It's me."

"WHAT?" yelled Ace.

"It's me," I repeated. "Zelly."

"SO, NU? IS THE DOOR BROKEN? COME IN."

I came in and put O.J. on the table next to Ace's TV-watching chair.

"Grandpa, I need to talk to you about O.J."

"SO TALK."

"Well, it's just, I've really tried. But, the thing is, I don't think this is going to work."

"WHAT'S NOT GOING TO WORK?" His eyes stayed on the screen. An old episode of *Star Trek* was on, which was no surprise since his favorite channel practically never shows anything else. Captain Kirk and Mr. Sulu were on the bridge, having a heated discussion.

"O.J. I just don't think my parents are going to go for it, no matter how long I keep doing this."

"NONSENSE," said Ace.

"Grandpa, I'm serious."

"WELL, WHAT DO YOU WANT ME TO DO ABOUT IT?"

"I dunno. I guess I was thinking we could call off the plan."

"CALL IT OFF? NO CAN DO."

"What do you mean?"

Ace finally turned away from the screen. He looked me right in the eye and said, "YOU CAN'T JUST STOP TAKING CARE OF SOMEONE BECAUSE YOU GET TIRED OF HIM. DOESN'T WORK THAT WAY." Then he went back to looking at the TV. On the screen, Mr. Spock stepped between Captain Kirk and Mr. Sulu. A Vulcan nerve pinch seemed imminent.

"Grandpa," I said. "Come on."

"WHERE ARE WE GOING?"

"Grandpa! O.J. isn't a real dog."

"SO HE'S A PRACTICE DOG. STILL, A DOG'S A DOG."

"Yeah, but no matter what you call it, it's made of plastic. It can go out with the recycling."

"IZZAT SO?" said Ace, clearly unmoved. "WELL, I GUESS IT'S A GOOD THING YOU DON'T HAVE A REAL DOG." He pulled out his ratty old handkerchief, blew his nose loudly into it, then stuffed it back into his pocket.

Now I was getting frustrated. Ace was acting like it was my fault I didn't have a real dog, when in fact his stupid plan just plain didn't work!

"I don't have a real dog," I said, "because I listened to you. Instead, I have a dumb old plastic jug with a face drawn on the side of it. Which doesn't wag its tail, or chase sticks, or do anything that a real dog does!"

"SO HE'S A LAZY DOG," said Ace. "WHADDAYA WANT FROM ME? YOU DON'T WANT TO TAKE CARE OF HIM ANYMORE? FIND HIM A NEW OWNER. YOU CAN'T JUST CALL IT QUITS."

On the TV, the credits started. Ace picked up his cane, aiming it at the buttons on the TV to change the channel because he doesn't trust the remote. I could tell that, to him, our conversation, just like his television program, was over. Case completely closed.

Well, maybe for Ace it was. But not for me. I planted myself firmly in front of his chair.

"How am I supposed to find him a new owner?" I asked. "He's an orange juice jug! Not a dog."

"THEN MAYBE YOU SHOULD KEEP HIM A LITTLE LONGER," said Ace indifferently, leaning to one side to keep the TV screen in view.

"Look, Grandpa," I explained, struggling to get through to him, "my parents are not going to change their mind and get me a dog, no matter what I do."

"FINE, SO GIVE UP. YOU KNOW WHAT YOUR PROBLEM IS, KID? NO PATIENCE. YOU WANT EVERY-THING YESTERDAY."

If my dad had been there, he probably would have dished out some of his Zen master wisdom. But he wasn't. And Ace was making me so mad I couldn't stop.

"You know what YOUR problem is?" I said, hearing my voice getting almost as loud as Ace's. "You think you're still a judge, but you're NOT! You're so busy being JUDGE ACE and bossing everyone around, but you don't care about any-one but yourself!" And then, because I couldn't help myself, I added, "Unlike Bubbles."

Ace took his eyes off the screen. He looked me straight in the eye, and it felt like he was going to explode. He got louder than ever. "YOUR GRANDMOTHER, MAY SHE REST IN PEACE, COULD TEACH YOU A THING OR TWO ABOUT PATIENCE. HER FAMILY CAME TO THIS COUNTRY WITH NOTHING. BUPKIS! THEY WORKED

THEIR FINGERS TO THE BONE JUST TO MAKE A LIFE HERE. ALL OF US DID."

"I know, I know," I said. Like the herring joke, I had heard this speech before. Many times.

"YOU KNOW," he said mockingly. "SHE KNOWS," he added, like he was telling someone else, even though there was nobody there. "DON'T TELL ME YOU KNOW, KID. YOU HAVE NO IDEA."

"I have no idea?" I yelled back. "YOU have no idea! This whole dumb O.J. thing is just some big joke to you, but it's NOT funny! It's my life!"

"YOUR GRANDMOTHER—" Ace started to continue.

"My grandmother," I interrupted, "wouldn't have let you do this to me! I wish—"

And I closed my mouth quick before my terrible thought— *I wish that it had been you instead of her!*—could come rolling out of my mouth. I grabbed O.J. by the handle, and instead, I yelled, "I wish I had never listened to you in the first place. The deal's off. I'm throwing this dumb thing away."

I ran out of Ace's room, stomped through the kitchen, and went out to the garage. I dumped O.J. into a dark green garbage can, his head leaning to one side and staring at me with that goofy grin.

Sorry, pal, I thought to myself, before slamming the lid on the can so I didn't have to look at him anymore. *Can't say I didn't try. I gave it my best shot.*

On my way back through the house, I practically collided with Sam, who was posing in the hall in his bathrobe,

brandishing a mop. Shortly after the Fourth of July, Sam had abruptly given up Batman and was now exclusively pretending to be Luke Skywalker.

"May the Force be with you," he said to me as I pushed past him and up the stairs.

"Great, I could use it," I said before slamming the door to my room.

CHAPTER 14

The next morning, when I came downstairs, there were five places set at the breakfast table as usual. What was unusual was that Ace's place setting was untouched.

"Where's Ace?" I asked my mom.

"He went to services," she answered.

"I thought he didn't go to temple anymore."

"So did I," she said, looking puzzled. "But today he got up early and asked to be taken. So your dad drove him."

I wondered whether Ace would see Jeremy at services. I pictured them sitting side by side: Ace and Ace Junior. I felt a pang of guilt at the thought, remembering how awful I had been to both of them. Especially Ace. Maybe that was the reason Ace decided to go back to services. He was probably telling God about me right now. The thought gave me a stomachache.

Just then, my dad wandered in, carrying a paper sack. "Your father," he said to my mom, "is a conundrum. However, get a load of this. I stopped by that new bakery after dropping him off." He set the bag down and pulled out a fat roll with a hole in the center.

"Is that supposed to be a bagel?" asked my mom, amused. Real bagels were high on the list of things my parents missed about New York.

"I think so," said my dad, biting into it eagerly. He made a disappointed face.

"At least they're trying," said my mom.

After breakfast, my parents insisted on dragging me and Sam along on another of their family outings. This time, we went shopping for gardening supplies for the vegetable patch my mom had started in our backyard. This took us to a big store called Garden Way. My parents had never grown vegetables before, so they had to call over people wearing bright green aprons and ask them questions about every little thing. They took us to Al's French Fries for lunch after, and then drove us to the lake for a swim, but it only barely made up for the hours of killing time in the Garden Way aisles.

"Do we have to pick up Ace?" I asked on the way home from the lake. "I mean, I need to get over to Allie's." I didn't exactly want to see Ace or have to answer any questions about O.J.'s whereabouts, but I sort of wanted to make sure he was still speaking to me.

"Relax," said my dad. "But, no, we don't need to collect Ace. He said he'd get himself home on the bus."

"What? I thought you said he was getting a ride," said my mom, turning toward my dad.

"He said he'd get himself home, and he will. He'll be fine, Lynn," said my dad, patting her knee. I could tell from the backseat that my mom was frowning. She worries about Ace more than my dad does.

By the time we got home, I barely had enough time to throw my sleeping bag and sleepover stuff in a bag and race to Allie's.

Ace's door was closed when I went by it. As usual, it claimed he had GONE FISHING. *I'll talk to him tomorrow*, I promised myself. I was already late. And besides, it would be better that way. It would give him time to calm down if he hadn't already.

When I got to Allie's, the other girls were already there. They turned out to be Megan O'Malley and Jenny Hood, both of whom were in our class and, it turned out, both of whom had gone to camp with Allie. They were in the middle of an argument about some dumb camp thing when I got there, which made me want to turn around and leave immediately. But I plunked myself down in a chair and told myself that at least Allie hadn't invited camp friends I didn't know. And at least I wouldn't have to think about apologizing to Ace—or Jeremy, for that matter—until the next morning.

We ended up having a pretty fun time watching movies

and eating popcorn and pizza in the Schmidt family's basement rec room. As usual, Allie's family had all sorts of stuff my mom never bought: soda, gummy bears, Twizzlers, and plain *and* peanut M&M's. And not just in the cupboard for sneaking. For the sleepover, Mrs. Schmidt set all the candy out for us in big glass bowls like a real party. Plus she made a whole pan of brownies just for us.

When Mrs. Schmidt finally came down with her Dustbuster to clean up the spilled popcorn and tell us it was time for bed, we all just spread our sleeping bags out on the carpeted floor of the rec room. But, of course, none of us had any intention of going to sleep.

"Let's have a séance!" suggested Megan.

Allie groaned. "No way," she said. "Remember the séance we did at camp? You guys were supposed to levitate me, but then you dropped me?"

"That wasn't my fault," protested Megan.

"Séances are dumb," interrupted Jenny. "Let's play Truth or Dare!"

"Not it!" yelled Allie and Megan at once, real fast.

"Jinx," said Jenny. Then we both laughed while Allie and Megan couldn't talk and made these pleading faces until Jenny finally unjinxed them.

"Okay," said Allie. "So, Zelly, you're it. Truth or dare?"

I hesitated. I hated dares. They usually ended up with having to prank-call a store or a boy from school. Or, worse, having to eat some disgusting concoction from the fridge like tuna salad with chocolate sauce. But truth, well, that had

its own problems. I mean, what if Allie asked me about Jeremy—or O.J., for that matter? Of course, she had promised she wouldn't, but what if she forgot?

"Truth," I finally said, staring hard at Allie like *You better not.*

"Okay, okay!" said Jenny, cradling her chin in her hands. Then she and Megan and Allie went to the end of the sofa and whispered. I sat in a pink beanbag chair, petting Lydia Potts, the Schmidt family's boulder of a cat.

Finally, giggling, Allie, Megan, and Jenny trooped over to me. Lydia Potts arched her back and dived the other way, trying to wedge herself under the sofa.

"The question is," said Allie, trying to keep a straight face, "which of the Sleuth brothers do you think is cuter? The *older* one? Or the *younger* one?"

"Allie!" I yelled. "You promised!"

"What?" she said defensively. "I'm not talking about *them.* I'm asking about the real Sleuth brothers. You know, from *The Brothers Sleuth?* The TV show? With Chaz Parker?"

"Not talking about who?" asked Jenny.

"And Zack Owens," added Megan. "Whenever there's danger," she sang, doing an exaggerated rendition of the theme song.

"I'll cover you, man!" Allie chimed in, trying to make her voice sound low like a guy's.

"'Cause you're my bro-ther . . . ," they crooned together.

"Wait, shut up, you guys. Not talking about *who?*" repeated Jenny.

"Nothing," I snapped. "I changed my mind. Dare."

"You can't do that," argued Jenny. "If you said truth, you have to do truth."

"Or what?"

"Or . . . you're out of the game," said Jenny.

"Yeah, and you have to go home," added Megan. "Right, Allison?"

I stared at Allie, who blinked several times, fast.

"Ummm . . . ," said Allie, stalling. She looked at Megan, then Jenny, before looking back at me.

I glared at her. Finally I said, "Joe."

"What?"

"Joe Sleuth."

"Zack Owens!" cried Megan triumphantly.

"Ugh, you guys are such babies," said Allie. "Anyone can see that Chaz Parker is *much* cuter."

I tried not to fume as Jenny and Megan both asked for and did dares. Then it was Allie's turn and she said truth. Jenny and Megan insisted they had the perfect question for her.

"Okay, who would you rather kiss?" said Jenny. "A dead frog covered with flies and maggots or—"

"Q-tip!" yelled Megan.

Allie shrieked. Megan and Jenny fell over, laughing.

"Who's Q-tip?" I asked, trying to remember if he was a character from some show.

Megan stopped laughing long enough to tell me. "He's this kid from camp. His real name's Curtis, but everyone

called him Q-tip because he's really skinny, but he has this giant puffball of frizzy hair."

"Like me?" I said, feeling angry again.

"Worse!" hollered Jenny. She must have realized how it sounded, because she quickly added, "I mean, your hair is really pretty, Zelly. His is a mess. Plus it's orange!"

"Yeah, he looks sort of like that kid Jeremy," said Allie. "Only with bright orange hair."

"Who's Jeremy?" asked Megan.

"He's that kid who moved into the Blanchards' house, right?" asked Jenny, a sneaky look coming across her face. "My mom took them some brownies. But his mom said they couldn't eat them because they weren't kosher."

"Seriously?" asked Megan.

"Uh-huh," said Jenny.

Everyone looked at me.

"How come you can eat brownies, but they can't?" asked Jenny. "You're Jewish too, right?"

"Yeah," I said warily. "But we're not kosher."

"You don't eat ham," said Allie.

"I don't *like* ham," I said. "That's different."

"Brownies aren't not kosher," scoffed Jenny. "My mom said she must have just made that up." Again, everyone looked at me like I was the authority.

"Yeah, well, I don't know about that," I said.

"Does Jeremy wear one of those little beanies?" asked Jenny.

"Those little what-ies?"

"Beanies," she repeated. "You know, those little hat thin-gies."

"You mean a yarmulke?" I asked. "No. He wears a Red Sox cap sometimes."

"Oh yeah? What else does he wear?"

"Jeremy? I dunno. Just regular clothes. Shorts, T-shirts, you know, and—" I suddenly noticed that Jenny looked like she was about to burst out laughing.

"What?" I said.

"Nothing!" Jenny replied. But she glanced at Megan, who looked like she knew exactly what Jenny was smirking about.

"What?" I asked, louder. Jenny tried to put on a super-innocent face, but Megan grabbed a pillow and whacked her with it, and then they both just started laughing and laughing.

"You guys, cut it out!" said Allie. She lunged for a bowl of jelly beans we had hidden under a beanbag chair so her mom wouldn't take them upstairs and held it protectively like Jenny and Megan were about to break a precious heirloom. But then she threw a handful of jelly beans at them and Jenny and Megan, shrieking, attacked her with pillows.

I hung back, not feeling like joining in. Finally, Allie threw a jelly bean at me. I made a fakey smile back.

"What's wrong?" she asked.

"Nothing," I said.

"No, seriously."

"I just . . ." I took a deep breath and looked at Jenny. "Why were you asking me all that stuff?"

"About what?"

"You know. About Jeremy?"

Jenny grinned mischievously. "Jeremy who?"

"JENNY!" said Allie. "Zelly, ignore her, she's just being dumb."

"Yeah," said Megan. "And even if he is your boyfriend, it's really okay."

"WHAT?" I yelled. "Who said that?"

Jenny and Megan looked at Allie.

"I did *not* say that!" said Allie. "I said they *look* like they should be boyfriend and girlfriend!"

"What's *that* supposed to mean?"

"Nothing! You just both have glasses and dark wavy hair and . . ."

I glared at Allie. "And?" I said.

"What? That's all. Honest!" she said.

"Do you swear?" I said suspiciously.

"You also said his brother was cute," added Megan.

"Chaz Parker–cute," threw in Jenny.

"Okay, but that's it, really. I swear, Zelly!" Allie gave me a pleading look.

Just then, I heard the door at the top of the basement stairs creak open. All of us froze.

"Zelly, honey?" I heard Allie's mom say. "The phone's for you. Can you come up here a minute?"

I gave Allie a final angry look before going up the stairs. Mrs. Schmidt was in her bathrobe and slippers. Her face looked oddly pale, maybe because she usually wears a lot of makeup. She put a hand on my shoulder and handed me the phone.

"Hello?" I said.

"Zelly, it's Daddy," said my dad. "Listen, I'm calling you from the hospital."

"What happened?" I said, my heart starting to pound.

"Everything is okay now," said my dad quickly, "but Ace had a heart attack. He's going to stay the night so they can monitor him and help him if he runs into any more trouble. We'll come get you in the morning, but I just wanted you to know what had happened. If you need to reach us before then, Mrs. Schmidt has the number for the hospital."

"But he was fine this morning," I said. Although as soon as I did, I realized that I hadn't actually seen him that morning. The last time I had seen him had been the night before. When I was yelling and screaming at him, just before I gave up on his plan and threw O.J. in the trash.

"Sam's here with us," continued my dad, like he was giving an oral report or something. "But I just called Paul's dad, and he's going to come get him."

I made a funny little noise in my throat.

"Zell? Are you okay?"

"I want to go home," I said.

CHAPTER 15

"What's wrong?" asked Allie when I came back downstairs and began stuffing my things back into my overnight bag.

"I have to go," I told her.

"What? Why?" said Allie.

"Who was on the phone?" asked Megan.

"Nobody," I told her. For some reason, my stuff wouldn't fit back in my bag, so I had to dump everything out on the carpet and start with the sleeping bag first. Focusing on this task was good because it kept me from crying.

"Would that be a Mr. Jeremy Nobody?" asked Jenny.

I gave the sleeping bag a final shove and stood up.

"Noooo," I said, trying to sound indifferent.

"Hey, Zelly, wait," pleaded Allie. "Don't go. We're sorry.

We were just messing with you, honest." She glared at Megan and Jenny, who both nodded on cue.

"It's not that, okay? I just— I have to go."

"You're mad."

"I'm *not* mad."

"Well, then what?"

"Look, it's not about that." For some reason, I didn't want to tell them about Ace. Maybe because they'd act all sorry for me and make a big deal. Maybe because after I left, they might talk about my weird grandpa and me even more. And Allie, who'd already broken her promise and told about Jeremy, might even break down and tell the others about just how crazy my weird grandpa was: *Get this: he made Zelly walk around the neighborhood dragging a plastic jug and pretending it was a dog . . . even cleaning up its pretend dog poop! NUH-uh! Yuh-HUH!*

"I just have to go," I finally said again.

"You said that," Allie replied, looking irritated and hurt, probably because I wouldn't explain.

I didn't know what else to say, so I started up the stairs to go wait for my dad.

"Hey, Allison," I heard Jenny say. "C'mere."

And then I heard whispering and laughing.

Later, Allison, I thought to myself.

I thought my dad was going to drive me to the hospital, but he took me home instead. He didn't say anything, he just turned left to go to our house instead of right to go to the

hospital and that was that. When we got home, he explained that he was going to stay with me, but my mom was going to spend the night at the hospital with Ace.

I was already wearing my pajamas, so I went up to my room, put my overnight bag down, and got into my bed. The house was really quiet, except for my dad's muffled voice downstairs. I guessed he was on the phone, calling over to the hospital. Which made me think about my conversation with Jeremy and what he had said about taking O.J. to the sleepover. *If they're really your friends, they won't make fun of you.* And what I had said to him. *Like you would know anything about that.*

Guilty tears stung my eyes. If anyone didn't have any friends, it was me. I couldn't believe I'd convinced myself that Jenny and Megan were my friends. And Allie, my so-called best friend, was the worst of all, breaking her promises and blabbing my secrets so everyone could laugh at me.

Well, fine. Who needed them? I had other friends. Like Jeremy, maybe, if he was still speaking to me after how mean I had been on the phone. And Lena, back in Brooklyn, although except for an occasional email I hadn't heard from her in months. She probably had a new best friend by now. A good one, not a traitor like Allie. *In the fall,* I told myself, *when sixth grade begins, I'm going to start over and make all new friends. Friends who I can trust. Friends who really understand me. Friends who are just like me.*

Oh, who was I kidding? No one here was just like me. Everyone was just like Allie and Megan and Jenny. Except

me, and Jeremy maybe, and Laraine Marcus, the only black girl in my class, who was almost six feet tall and never said a word to anyone. *Fine*, I thought to myself, *forget about people friends*. One of these days, I'd convince my parents to get me a real dog instead of O.J. and then he could be my one true friend.

O.J.

Oh no.

All of a sudden, I remembered what I had done. My heart started pounding. I had thrown O.J. in the trash. I had yelled at Ace. I had told Ace that I was done with O.J. and Ace's stupid old plan.

And then he had a heart attack.

Just like that.

Oh God.

What had I done?

I jumped out of bed. I tiptoed downstairs in my pajamas and opened the front door. The cold night air made the hair on my arms stand up, but I didn't hesitate. I ran outside, barefoot.

I was afraid that if I opened the big, rolling garage door, my dad might hear me, so I crept into the garage through the side door. It was really dark, so I went back into the house and found a flashlight in the junk drawer by the phone. With the flashlight, I reentered the garage and went over to the trash cans. I lifted the lid of the first one and found . . .

Ewww! The pungent, sweet smell of overripe bananas, dirty coffee grounds, and moldy leftovers bombarded me.

Slam!

Garbage. No O.J.

I moved over to the other can. Lifting the lid with one hand and plugging my nose with the other, I peeked inside. . . .

Empty.

Oh no.

Where was O.J.?

Was it possible he was in the first can, buried under the trash on top? I had thrown him out more than a day earlier. Much as I didn't like this possibility, there was only one way to know. With the flashlight, I found one of the gardening trowels we had bought at Garden Way. I also put on my mom's new gardening gloves, even though I knew I'd be in big trouble if they ended up getting stinky.

Using the trowel, I picked through the trash. Tossing some of the larger items—like milk cartons, wadded-up paper towels, and a cereal box—in the empty garbage can gave me room to dig deeper.

After shoveling my way through about half of the full can of garbage, I still hadn't found O.J. To make it easier, I picked up the half-full can and tried to dump it into the formerly empty—

"What in the world?"

"Augh!!!" The sound of my dad's voice startled me and made me jump. My grip on the trash can loosened and it began to fall, at which point my dad lurched forward to try to steady it—

And I ended up dumping out the rest of the garbage. All over my dad's feet. And my own.

Lucky for him, he was wearing slippers. The cold, slimy mess squished between my bare toes.

"Zelly, what in God's name are you doing?!" yelled my dad. So much for the Zen master.

"It's all my fault!" I confessed, the truth bursting out of me like soda when you shake it up. "I got mad at Grandpa and quit O.J. and threw him out and it's all my fault!" And then I just started crying. "I'm sorry," I managed to choke out between sobs.

My dad leaned down, right there in the garbage with me, and put his arms around me.

"It's going to be okay," he told me.

I started to talk, to protest, but he shushed me, very softly, again and again, like I remember him doing when I was really little and I fell down and hurt myself.

"It's okay. It's going to be okay," he said again.

And I cried some more and hugged him back.

Because I really, really wanted to believe him.

The next morning, my dad made breakfast for the two of us. He made some extra toast and wrapped it in foil and packed a thermos of coffee to bring to my mom, who had spent the night at the hospital.

We ate together, not talking. I was grateful that he didn't mention the mess with O.J. and the garbage. I was grateful to my dad for a lot of things. The night before, after I had

stopped crying, he had run me a bath. Then, later on, as I was drifting off to sleep, he had come into my room and kissed me and petted my hair. After breakfast, when we went out to get in the car to drive to the hospital, I noticed that he had also cleaned up all the garbage.

Unfortunately, there was still no sign of O.J.

When we got to the hospital, the way it smelled made me feel like throwing up. It reminded me of the times we visited Bubbles there before she died.

Please don't let him die, I thought to myself as we went up in the elevator. I guess it was like praying, although I don't usually do that so I didn't think anyone would actually be listening. If that's how it works, that you have to have a relationship with God in order to ask for stuff. Although, now that I thought about it, it seemed like maybe God wouldn't be that way. Maybe God would be nice enough to listen to anyone in need, not just people who had done everything you're supposed to do, like joining a temple and saying real prayers and all that.

Okay, God, I tried again, *if you're out there, please don't let Ace die. I'll do whatever you want, okay? I'll walk O.J. until I'm a hundred and three if I have to.*

Except O.J. is gone, I suddenly remembered. Well, maybe I could make a new O.J. out of another old orange juice jug. In kindergarten, my class had a pet hamster named Timmy, and it wasn't until Sam started kindergarten in the same classroom that I realized that it had to be, like, Timmy the Seventeenth by then. *Even if I have to make a new O.J. to do*

it, *I will*, I promised God. *Just let Ace be okay. Ace is my grandpa*, I added, just in case God needed some sort of explanation of who I was talking about. Which he probably didn't, since he's God, but I figured it couldn't hurt.

When the elevator doors opened, we stepped out into a hallway. "Here we are," said my dad, in this phony happy voice I remembered him using when we had visited Bubbles there. To the right, there was some sort of lounge area, with light green walls and peachy pink couches.

I followed my dad down the hall to a tall desk, where a bunch of people in hospital clothes were standing around. My dad told the lady behind the desk Ace's name, and the lady told him to wait. She left the desk and went down the hall and came back with my mom.

"Hi, sweetie," she said, and I hugged her. "Grandpa's resting now."

"Can I see him?"

"Let's let him get some rest. He had a rough night."

"Is he going to be okay?" I asked.

My mom took off her glasses and rubbed her eyes. "Well, if anyone can get through something like this, he can. As Ace will be the first to tell you, he's a tough old bird."

"Why don't you go to the family waiting area," suggested the lady who had been behind the desk. She looked eager to get us out of the hallway.

"Okay," said my mom, and the three of us walked over to where the pink couches were.

"Did you get any sleep?" my dad asked her.

154

My mom shook her head. "The monitors went off a bunch of times during the night. And one time, the nurses didn't come in, so I had to run out and get them. After that, I couldn't even doze off."

"What happened?" I asked.

My mom sighed and began talking like I was a little kid asking why the sky was blue or something. "Oh, there are just these medical machines that the doctors use to monitor Ace's vital signs—"

"No, Mom," I interrupted her. "What happened to him? What made him end up here in the first place?"

"Oh," said my mom. "Didn't Daddy tell you? Ace had a heart attack."

"Yes, I know," I said. "I mean, what made him have a heart attack?" Ace always said that my dad's jogging was going to give him a heart attack. But Ace didn't jog. He didn't even play golf anymore.

"It doesn't work that way, sweetie," said my dad. "I mean, yes, something can trigger a heart attack, or it can just happen out of a clear blue sky."

"For someone Ace's age, that is," added my mom quickly. "You don't have to worry that it is going to happen to you."

"I know," I told her. "I'm not six, remember?" *So stop talking to me like you do to Sam,* I added in my head.

"Hey, do we need to go get Sam?" My mom turned to my dad like she had read my mind.

"No, Frank Harwood said they'd keep him through dinner."

My mom looked relieved.

"Are you hungry?" she asked me. I shrugged. If it got me out of sitting in the lounge with the pink couches, I was. "Why don't we go take a walk to the cafeteria?" she asked. "Nate, can you stay with Ace?"

"Sure," said my dad, picking up a magazine and walking back toward the lady and her desk.

At the hospital cafeteria, I picked out a donut and a carton of chocolate milk, and my mom didn't even frown. That's how unlike herself she was. We sat and she had coffee and I ate, and neither of us said anything until I was practically done.

Finally, almost as if she was talking to another mom or something, my mom said, "I hate hospitals."

"Me too," I told her.

"I always did, even before my mo— I mean, when Grandma got sick, that really did it for me."

"Is Ace going to be okay?" I asked again.

My mom was quiet for a second. Then she said, "I hope so."

"I don't want him to die," I admitted.

"Of course not, sweetie," she said. "No one does."

"Yeah, but"—this was the hard part—"promise you won't be mad?" She nodded, so I told her, "I kind of wished for it. I didn't mean it," I added quickly. "I just got so mad at him. I also yelled at him. A lot." My eyes welled up with tears again.

"Zelly, sweetie, listen to me," my mom said, holding both of my hands firmly. "You did not cause this. You can't make someone have a heart attack."

"Okay," I said.

"You can't," she repeated. "I told Sam that and I'll tell you."

"Sam? What did Sam say?"

"Oh, Sam thought Grandpa had a heart attack because you told Jeremy about O.J. Any idea where he got that idea?" She raised one eyebrow.

I looked down at my tray. "I'm sorry," I said.

"I know you are," she said.

"But Daddy said if Grandpa's blood pressure gets raised, like by arguing, it can make him sick."

"What Daddy probably meant is that sometimes people have heart attacks because something put too much strain on their hearts, like stress or smoking." She looked irritated. I wasn't sure if it was at me or at him. "But sometimes," she continued, "people, especially older people like Grandpa, just have heart attacks for no reason."

"Okay," I said doubtfully.

"Zelly, it's true." She locked eyes with me. "You didn't cause this. All right?"

"All right," I said, even though I wasn't sure whether to believe her or not. I had a feeling that the only person who might tell it to me straight would be Ace. Say what you will about Ace, he's not known for pulling his punches to make people feel better.

"Hey, how was Allie's slumber party?" my mom asked suddenly, like she had forgotten.

"It was okay," I said.

"Just okay?"

"Well, I didn't actually end up sleeping over."

"I know. Daddy told me. What happened?"

"Well, when he called to tell me about Grandpa, I just wanted to come home."

"Okay."

"But . . . the thing is, it wasn't so great even before that," I admitted.

"Oh no?"

And so I told her about Allie and Jenny and Megan and the way they were acting about Jeremy.

"And they kept calling her *Allison*." I rolled my eyes. "And they wouldn't stop teasing me about Jeremy."

My mom looked amused. "Really?" she asked.

"Yes," I told her. "They kept acting like Jeremy and I are going to have to get married because we supposedly look like each other and we both have glasses. And we're both Jewish."

"Oh, right," said my mom, nodding. "Because all Jewish people are required to marry other Jewish people."

"No, they're not," I said. "Wasn't one of Daddy's parents not Jewish?"

"Yup," said my mom. "Grandpa Bill."

"Right! So, why did those guys have to say all that stuff?"

"Zelly," my mom said lightly, "it sounds like your friends were just teasing. Or, at worst, being a little ignorant."

"It's not just that, though." I sighed. "I feel like I could live here forever, but I'd never really fit in. Nobody else looks like me here. Nobody else's brother dressed up like Batman

on the Fourth of July. And nobody else ever unwrapped her lunch and found a sandwich made out of a *cow's tongue*."

My mom smiled sadly at the memory. "I stopped letting Ace pack your lunch after that."

"You're sure he's going to be okay, right?" I asked suddenly. All this talk about me and my problems made me forget for a minute the reason we were here. I felt a pang of guilt for complaining about being teased while Ace was upstairs fighting for his life. I might not even get the chance to see him again. Or to tell him how sorry I was.

"I hope so, sweetie," said my mom.

"Me too," I said. And meant it.

My mom took a sip of her coffee, then said, "Ace really does mean well. Did I ever tell you about the time my mom was having a problem with this neighbor of ours?"

It took a second for me to realize she was talking about Bubbles. Usually, she called them Bubbles and Ace, or "your grandma and grandpa," not "my mom and dad."

"No," I said. "What was the problem?"

"He was just a really unpleasant person, from what I recall. He was a big joker, and he always had something kind of nasty to say at someone else's expense. Anyhow, one day he said something that upset my mom more than usual. Probably some sort of insensitive joke or prejudiced remark. And let me tell you, my mom was hopping mad."

"Wow," I said. It was impossible to picture Bubbles, with her broad smile and paint-spattered sneakers, getting mad at anyone.

"When my mom told Ace what the neighbor had said," continued my mom, "I expected him to march next door to give him a lecture. You know how Ace can be."

I nodded. Did I ever.

"And you know what he did?"

I shook my head.

"He said, 'INVITE HIM TO DINNER.'" My mom imitated Ace's booming voice. "'*To dinner?*' asked my mom. 'TO SHABBES DINNER,' said my dad. '*Abraham, have you lost your mind?*' asked my mom. '*Why would we invite that shmendrick into our home?*' And Ace said, 'YOU GOTTA START SOMEWHERE.'"

"Ace said that?" I asked.

My mom nodded proudly. "Do you know why he's called Ace?" she asked.

"Because his last name is Diamond, right?" I said. "They used to call him 'Judge Ace' or 'the Ace of Diamonds' or something?"

My mom put her purse on the table and started digging through it. Eventually, she pulled out a worn-looking box of playing cards with an old-fashioned design and the word *Bicycle* in red at the top.

"One of the nurses gave me these to help pass the time," she explained. She shrugged. "Solitaire, I guess she was thinking."

She opened the box at one end and spread all the cards out on the table. She pushed them around until she found the card she was looking for. It had a big red diamond shape in

the center, with two letter A's and small diamond shapes in two of the corners.

"Here it is. The ace of diamonds," she said, holding it up.

"Right," I said.

"You know that in cards, an ace is worth one point, right?" she said.

I nodded. I suddenly remembered Ace playing Go Fish with me when I was little. And Crazy Eights and some game he called Rummy. I used to love to watch him shuffle, *whirrrrr*, like a machine. When I tried to do it myself, the cards would go flying everywhere.

"But here's the thing," she added. "An ace can also be worth eleven points, which is more than any other card, even a king or queen. So an ace is called a 'wild' card, which makes it the best card in the deck."

My mom handed the ace of diamonds to me, then gathered up the rest of the cards while she talked. "When Grandpa was a judge," she continued, "the lawyers in his courtroom called him 'the Ace of Diamonds.' You're right that the 'diamond' part was because of his last name. The 'ace' part was because he was a little 'wild,' a little unpredictable. Always full of surprises, your grandpa."

"I'll say," I said, studying the playing card and thinking about the day O.J. first appeared on my bedside table. I remembered Ace's mysterious note strapped in place with one of his beloved rubber bands.

She knocked the pile of cards against the table and began to slide them back into the box before continuing. "But you

know something, Zelly? They also called him 'Judge Ace' for another reason. And that was because, without fail, Grandpa always came through for people. That's just how he was—the best card in the deck."

"*Is*," I corrected her, handing her the ace.

My mom looked up, startled.

"You're right," she said, forcing a smile and sliding the ace back into the box. "Is."

CHAPTER 16

I wasn't allowed to see Ace at all that day. My mom asked if I wanted her to call Allie's mom or maybe Jeremy's mom to come get me, but I said no. I just wanted to stay at the hospital. She looked like she wanted to say something, but she didn't.

My mom spent the day going back and forth between Ace's room and the waiting room. My dad and I spent the day on the pink couches, flipping through old magazines and watching hours of television. I got to eat all kinds of things out of the vending machine: a silver bag of tiny potato chip sticks, a 3 Musketeers bar, a box of Cracker Jack, and some gummy snacks made with ten percent real fruit juice. My dad had a lot of loose change, and my mom wasn't there much to say no.

The next day was mostly the same, except Sam came to the hospital with us. In the middle of the afternoon, Ace's doctor told my mom he was stable enough for visitors. But only one visitor at a time. My mom apparently didn't count, which was good because I didn't like the idea of being alone in a hospital room with Ace. What if all of a sudden a machine went off or he stopped breathing or something?

My dad said I could go first. My mom took me down the long hall, past the desk with the lady behind it, to Ace's room. We entered the room and found Ace propped up in a hospital bed. He had a skinny rubber tube taped under his nose and more tubes taped to his arms and his chest.

His caterpillar eyebrows twitched when he saw me.

"Hiya, kid," he said. Only not in his usual booming Ace voice. More of a harsh, gravelly whisper.

"Hi, Grandpa," I said. I wasn't sure if I should get too close, but I saw his brown-spotted hand beckoning to me, so I shuffled forward. My mom pulled a chair over for me, and I sat down next to him. For the first time ever, Ace took my hand. Bubbles always did that with me in the hospital. "*Shayna velt*, your hands are so cold!" she would say. Always worrying about me, though she was the one who was so sick she didn't even have hair anymore.

Without meaning to, I started to cry.

"Sha, sha," said Ace, squeezing my hand. I wiped the tears away with my free hand. "It's gonna be all right. *Zorg zikh nisht*. I'm a tough old bird."

I took a deep breath. "I'm sorry I yelled at you."

Ace smiled, even though it looked like it hurt to do so. "In all my years on the bench," he said, "if I had a nickel for every time I got yelled at . . ." He whistled the tune of "If I Were a Rich Man" from *Fiddler on the Roof*.

"I'm still sorry," I said.

"You feel guilty?" he said. "Good! As your grandmother would say, my work is done."

"Bubbles?" I asked, confused. "But she never made me feel guilty."

"Not you, kiddo. She used to say that to me."

"You?" I remembered how my mom had said that Bubbles was the boss. But I didn't know that Bubbles. The Bubbles I knew was part fairy, my magic grandma with the sun in her hair and the pocketful of treasures.

"Sure," he said. "A grouchy bear like me, kvetching from morning till night? Ranting to anyone who'll listen? Who wouldn't lose her temper?"

A lone tear darted down Ace's cheek. It happened so fast I almost missed it. Ace swatted it away like a fly.

"I miss her," I told him.

"Of course you do," he said matter-of-factly. "You miss her, I miss her. The world misses her."

I nodded. It was exactly like that. He didn't say it like "You and everybody else." He said it like "The world is a sadder place without her in it."

"Ace—?" I began again.

"And another thing," he cut me off. "I've been thinking maybe it's time for 'Ace' to be retired."

"But aren't you already retired?"

"I'm retired from the bench, yes," said Ace. "So I'm thinking maybe it's enough with the 'Ace' business, already. Maybe I could try being plain old 'Grandpa.'"

"I don't want a plain old grandpa," I told him.

"Or I could try a new nickname," he said. "I'm thinking maybe 'Ambassador.'"

I smiled at his joke, but I knew I still had to say what I was going to say. "I'm also sorry I let you down." Before he could say anything, I continued, talking fast to get it over with. "I threw O.J. out. But I wish I didn't, and not just because you got sick. I should've kept my promise, and I wish I could go back and start all over again. So, you don't need to change. It's me who should have done things different."

Ace looked unimpressed. He waved one hand while still gripping mine tightly with his other hand.

"Tell it to him."

"To him?"

"Yup."

"To . . . God?" I whispered.

Ace chuckled softly, which looked like maybe it hurt. Then he began coughing and had a tough time stopping. I looked over at my mom, who was perched on the edge of her chair, ready to run out and grab a nurse if necessary. Ace coughed one more time, then waved his hand at her to show her he was okay.

"No, Zeldaleh. Tell it to O.J."

I was surprised to hear him call me something other than

"kid." I was also surprised that he hadn't heard what I said about O.J. Maybe his hearing aid wasn't in.

"But, Ace," I said louder, "I just told you . . ."

Ace smiled, that same satisfied smile from the herring-on-the-wall joke. He crooked one finger to get me to lean in. "You know what your problem is? You think too much." For the first time, he didn't say it accusingly. Instead, it sounded like he was confiding in me. "I know we can pull this off," he hissed urgently. "So all that matters"—he tapped my forehead and looked me straight in the eye—"is right in here. And," he added, poking me just below my collarbone, "a little in here."

"Okay . . . ," I said uncertainly, because I wasn't entirely sure what he was talking about. My *head and my heart?* I looked at the clear fluid in a bag hanging from a pole next to Ace's bed. Every few seconds, it would drip into the tube connected to his arm. I wondered if the medicine in it was making him loopy. Loopier than usual, that is.

Then he leaned his neck a little farther forward and crooked his finger again. I leaned in, so close I felt his hot breath on my ear.

"Look inside—" he whispered, but then he started coughing again, right in my ear. I pulled away, and he coughed some more, louder this time.

Just then, one of the machines started beeping and a nurse came running in. She sort of pushed me aside, and my mom came over and put her hands on my shoulders. The nurse punched some buttons on the machine and got it to stop beeping, which was a big relief. Ace was still coughing,

though, and trying to catch his breath. The nurse kind of nodded at my mom, who swung me out into the hall. In a few minutes, the nurse came out and told my mom that it would be good for Ace to get some more rest. Then she went back in, and we went down the hall to the waiting area.

My dad and Sam were sitting there, watching a game show. When Sam saw us, he jumped up. As usual, Sam was wearing his Jedi knight bathrobe. Tucked into the belt was a long plastic tube. It had tinfoil attached to one end, presumably to give his lightsaber a handle. Costume or no costume, Sam looked nothing like Luke Skywalker. He looked like a tired, frizzy-haired little kid wearing his bathrobe in the daytime. To top it off, he had a whole bunch of rubber bands on both wrists like bracelets. He had put them on "for luck" when my dad told him about Ace's heart attack, and now he refused to take them off.

"My turn!" said Sam. My mom squatted down next to him and gave him a hug.

"Next time, champ, okay? Ace needs some rest."

Sam stomped his foot on the ground hard. He crossed his arms emphatically, and his lightsaber slipped from his bathrobe and clattered to the floor, jarring the tinfoil handle loose.

"No fair!" he yelled.

"Sorry, kiddo. Doctor's orders," said my mom.

"Why does she get to go see him and I don't? She's the one who made his heart get attacked in the first place!"

"Sammy, we talked about that," my dad reminded him.

"Remember, it doesn't work that way. No one made Ace get sick."

"Yeah, but—" Sam started to say, but my dad scooped him up, just like he used to do when Sam was really little. My mom picked up the plastic tube and the tinfoil.

"It's been a long day," said my dad quietly. "How's about we go get dinner at Sally's?"

At the sound of the word *Sally's,* Sam hesitated. I could tell he really wanted to make a big, noisy scene so he could get his way and visit Ace. But Sam loved Sally's Pizza, with its free soda refills and bowling-pin-shaped balloons with cardboard feet. Sam nodded slowly, defeated. He put his head down on my dad's shoulder as we left the building.

In the backseat of the car coming home from Sally's, I could see that Sam was almost falling asleep.

"Sam?" I whispered.

"Hmmm?"

"I'm sorry I said that stuff about how telling would make Ace sick. Okay?"

"Uh-huh," he said.

He was quiet for another moment. Then he said, "My lightsaber broke."

"Yeah," I said. "You want me to fix it for you?"

"No," he said sadly. "It'll never be the same."

"I could try," I suggested.

Sam didn't say anything. I guess he must have fallen asleep. But when he sort of toppled over sideways so he was leaning on me, I didn't push him off.

That night, when we got home from the hospital, I went up to my room and thought about what Ace had said.

What did he mean, "Look inside"? Did he mean it like some sort of spiritual thing, like "Look in your heart"? That didn't sound like the Ace I knew. Although he had gone to temple the day of his heart attack. But then why would he have said he wasn't talking about God when he said, "Tell it to him"?

Maybe Jeremy would know. I decided to go talk to him in the morning. I owed him an apology anyway, and maybe he'd help me sort out some of Ace's cryptic comments. He was smart that way. And a good listener. Plus, with going to Hebrew school and everything, it seemed like Jeremy might have a direct line to God. I imagined Jeremy flipping open a special talk-to-God device, sort of like the communicators they use on *Star Trek*.

Just then, I heard the doorbell ring. It was almost like Jeremy had read my mind. My dad called, "Zelly!"

I ran downstairs. But instead of Jeremy, Allie was standing there.

"Hi," she said.

"Hi," I replied coolly, trying not to let her know that I was happy to see her.

"I called you like a million times, but there was no answer, so my mom said I could come by and leave you a note. She told me about your grandpa. I'm really sorry."

Allie handed me a piece of paper. It was folded up and had the words *To Zelly* and *Top Secret* written on the outside. I unfolded it and read:

> Dear Zelly,
> I'm really sorry about your grandpa. I hope he gets better soon. I'm also sorry you left my slumber party. My mom says you can sleep over again soon. I hope you want to.
>
> Your BFF,
Allie
> P.S. I'm actually going to stick with "Allie."

"I'll ask my mom," I told her cautiously. I didn't want to tell her that I didn't want to sleep over with Jenny and Megan anytime soon.

"Just you and me, okay?" said Allie.

"Okay," I said.

CHAPTER 17

The next morning, I walked over to Jeremy's house. Seth answered the door, then yelled into the house, "Hey, Germ-y. It's your GIRL-friend."

Jeremy came to the doorway but didn't open the screen.

"What do you want?" he said.

"Um, to say hi? Maybe to take a walk?"

"Oh, I don't know. What if your friends see you with me? Won't that keep you from running for Miss Popularity?"

"Jeremy, come on. I'm sorry, okay?"

"Hmph," said Jeremy. He didn't say anything else. And he still didn't open the screen door.

"So? Will you take a walk with me? Please?"

Jeremy opened the screen door. "I'll be back in a little bit," he yelled over his shoulder.

We started down toward the dead end, just like I always used to do with O.J.

"Where's O.J.?" asked Jeremy.

I sighed. "It's a long story," I told him.

I held my breath, waiting for Jeremy to say what he would have been perfectly entitled to say. Something like, *Let me guess. You gave O.J. up? You decided it was too hard, standing up to your friends, and you didn't want a dog that bad after all?*

But what Jeremy said was: "I've got time."

So I told him the whole story. Arguing with Ace and throwing O.J. in the trash and Allie's slumber party and getting the call about Ace's heart attack and trying to get O.J. back and the garbage everywhere and what Ace said when I told him about O.J.

"Wow," he said when I finished. "I had no idea your grandpa had heart problems. My grandpa had heart problems. He died when I was just a baby."

"My grandpa doesn't have heart problems," I informed him. "And he's a tough old bird. He's not going to die."

"No, I wasn't saying that. I just— Wow." Jeremy looked really overwhelmed by everything I had said.

"So, what do you think?"

"About what?"

"About what he said. About looking inside, and sticking with the plan even though O.J.'s gone, and 'Tell it to him.' Do you have any idea what he meant?"

"Not really. How would I know? He's your grandpa."

"Jeremy!" I was beginning to get frustrated. "Don't you go to temple and Hebrew school and everything?"

"Yeah? So?"

"Well, I guess I just thought maybe there was some sort of, I don't know, explanation for what he meant. You know, a Jewish explanation."

Jeremy looked dubious. "A Jewish explanation? I thought your grandpa didn't go to synagogue."

"He didn't. I mean, he hadn't been in ages. But get this: on the day he had the heart attack, he had gone to temple that morning."

"Weird."

"Hey, you went to temple on Saturday morning, right? Did you see him there?"

Jeremy shook his head. "Maybe he was at the other temple," he suggested. "The one my mom thinks we should check out next."

"There's another temple?"

"Yeah, there's actually three. One Reform, which is where we went on Saturday, one Conservative, and one Orthodox. They're not very big congregations, but my mom says some people drive in from way out in the country to attend services."

This *is the country*, I thought to myself. But then I pictured the real country landscapes of places outside Burlington, like the farm where we went to pick cherries. What if that girl I saw playing with her dogs was actually Jewish? And what if

her family got up extra-early every Saturday morning to drive to Burlington to attend services? What if I had this little tiny piece of me in common with her, and with kids like her, kids I hadn't even met?

"How was it?" I asked Jeremy.

"I liked it okay," he said, "but my mom didn't. There was this young rabbi who was in charge of the kids' portion of the service. He actually had us sing the Shema to the tune of the theme from *Star Wars*."

"He did what?"

"You know the Shema? It's a really basic Hebrew prayer that you sing. Only not usually like this." Jeremy launched into his imitation of the rabbi: "SHMA-ah yi-is-ra-EH-el . . ."

I chuckled. "Sam would like that."

"Yeah, well, me too. My mom, not so much."

"Big surprise."

Jeremy smiled. I felt relieved that he wasn't still mad at me. As we walked by the Brownells' house, I saw Maddy and Luna watching us through the window. *Where's that other dog?* Luna seemed to say. *You know, the funny-looking one?*

I wish I knew, I told her.

"Jeremy?" I said suddenly. "Can I ask you something?"

"Sure," said Jeremy.

I hesitated. I had just finished apologizing to him, and now here I was wanting him to trust me all over again. But this was important. I really needed to know. Finally, I blurted out, "What did you do to get your bike?"

Jeremy eyed the ground. "Nothing," he mumbled.

"Jeremy, please. I promise not to tell."

"Yeah, I don't know." He looked at me suspiciously.

"I said I was sorry, didn't I? And come on, it's because of my grandpa. I know it might sound crazy but I feel like if I can get O.J. back and stick to our plan, it'll help, maybe."

Jeremy kept staring at me. Finally he said, "If you tell anyone, I will *never* speak to you again."

"I promise! Not even Allie."

"Okay," he said. And then, "I gave up my thumb."

"You did what?"

Jeremy didn't answer. Instead, he held out his thumb for me to see. I had never noticed, but on the knuckle there was a hard, round bump.

"For real?" I almost laughed. "Like, *recently*?"

"Did you ever used to?"

"Suck my thumb? I mean, sure, I guess. When I was little."

"Yeah, well, if you don't stop then, it's totally different. It kind of becomes part of you. And then it's practically impossible to give up. My parents would've done anything to get me to quit."

"Wow. You must have really wanted that bike."

"Yeah," said Jeremy simply. "I didn't want to give up my thumb, but it was the only way I knew I could get my parents to take me seriously. They thought Seth's old bike was fine for me, even though it got loaned to my cousin one summer. And she put these dumb stickers all over it."

"Oof!" I said, making a face.

"Yeah, that's why I think you have to really own the whole O.J. thing. Take him everywhere, walk every dog in town, let everyone know you mean business. That's the only way it's going to work."

"Yeah, well, maybe," I said. *Of course*, I thought, *it would be a lot easier if I hadn't thrown him out.*

"Zell," said Jeremy softly, "you know, right, that even if you do all that, your grandpa still might—"

"La la la, I can't hear you," I yelled, running ahead with my hands over my ears.

Before Jeremy could catch up with me, I reached the dead end, the spot where I had scooped O.J.'s pretend poop all those times. As I cleared the corner of the hedge, I half expected to find O.J. sitting there, like some real dog that had slipped under a fence and run off to its favorite spot.

When my dad took us to the hospital so he could trade places with mom that afternoon, we came out of the elevator and found her sitting all by herself in the hall.

"Lynn . . . ?" said my dad carefully, and the way he said it made my stomach lurch: just like Bubbles all over again.

But my mom looked up and sort of smiled weakly.

"Still hanging in there," she said. "He's resting right now. And he complained about one of the nurses, which I'm taking as a good sign."

"Attaboy, Ace," said my dad.

Just then, my mom said, "I almost forgot. I have something for you, Zelly." Out of her pocket, she took a small, folded-up piece of paper.

"Ace wrote this note after you left yesterday. He was very emphatic that I make sure you got it."

My mom handed me the note.

I unfolded it and read what Ace had written. It said:

DEAR ZELDA,
LOOK INSIDE
MY CLOSET.
   LOVE,
   GRANDPA (ACE)

I started to laugh. I could tell that as he wrote it, Ace was smiling his satisfied smile, like when he'd tell that herring joke of his.

My mom peeked over my shoulder at the note. "What does it mean?" she asked me.

"I'll tell you later," I said, because I had an idea. As soon as I got home, I would find out for sure.

When we got home, I went straight to Ace's room. Without stopping to knock at the GONE FISHING sign, I grabbed the rubber-band-covered doorknob and threw open the door. There was his bed, his nightstand, his dresser, his bookcase, the cane he was supposed to use but didn't, his TV and TV chair, and . . .

His closet.

When I looked inside, I saw wide-lapelled jackets and overcoats, dress shirts, and even a tuxedo. There were plastic garment bags where he kept his long black judge's robes "for posterity." On the ground were pairs and pairs of spikeless golf shoes and two pairs of bedroom slippers.

And peeking out from behind the shoes, in the very back, I saw:

O.J.

Looking a little dirty and a tiny bit dented, but always, always smiling.

"What took you so long?" his smile seemed to say.

"I'm sorry," I told him. "I won't ever let you down again."

And he smiled. Because he knew I wouldn't.

And I smiled back because I knew I wouldn't.

CHAPTER 18

The next day, Allie stopped by. She wanted to see if I could walk with her to the Dairy Barn. Allie and I both loved the Dairy Barn, which was an ice cream stand you could get to by cutting through the University of Vermont campus.

"Can you do that?" she whispered at the door, looking nervous.

"Sure, why not?"

"My mom said your mom said something about how your family might be sitting and shivering for a few days."

I smiled. "It's called 'sitting shiva,'" I corrected her, "but you only do it if the person dies."

Ace hadn't come home from the hospital yet. But he hadn't died yet, either. Although you wouldn't know it—with all his friends and our neighbors stopping by and bring-

ing us food, it was practically like a funeral. I remembered how, at Bubbles' shiva, Ace had gone around yelling, "ENOUGH WITH THE DANISH, ALREADY! THERE'S ENOUGH CHAZERAI HERE TO FEED AN ARMY." *Sorry, Ace,* I thought. *Looks like you're going to have to put up with Danish a little while longer.*

"Lemme see if I can escape, okay?" I told Allie.

Allie waited on my front steps while I got permission to go out for a little while. However, when I came out of the house with O.J., she gave me a funny look.

"Um, Zell? What are you doing?"

"Bringing O.J.," I said. "He needs a walk."

"But I thought you were only doing that because your grandpa made you," said Allie.

"I was, at first. But not anymore. Do you have a problem with that?"

"No."

"Because I don't care what people— You don't?"

Allie's eyes narrowed. "Of course not. Why would I?"

"Uh, I don't know," I said. "I thought you thought it was embarrassing."

"Yeah, I did," she admitted. "But so did you."

"True," I said.

"If you're okay with it now, I guess I should be too. I mean, we're best friends, right?"

It made my heart jump for joy to hear her say that. But I still wanted to make sure. "So, you're not going to insist that I put him in a grocery bag or something?" I asked.

"Can you?" she asked hopefully.

I considered the idea, remembering how, in the City, some dogs got carried around in purses. But then I thought of what Ace had said about treating O.J. like a real dog. And in Vermont, dogs have to walk.

"I don't think so," I told her.

"Oh well," she said. "It was worth a shot."

So I hooked O.J.'s leash on him, and the three of us set off for the Dairy Barn. Since most of the route was on the university's grassy campus, O.J. was quiet enough for us to almost forget he was along.

Until we were in line at the Dairy Barn.

I was pretty sure I was going to get black raspberry. Allie was staring at the board, fidgeting with her money.

"You know you want a creemee," I told her. I used to say *soft serve*, which is what they call it in New York, but now it doesn't even cross my mind.

"Yeah, but chocolate or twist?" said Allie.

Then all of a sudden we heard . . .

"Hey, do you SMELL something?"

I turned, and who was standing there grinning meanly at me but Nicky Benoit.

My heart started pounding, but I took a deep breath. In my head, I could hear Jeremy saying, *Don't let him see that he bothers you.*

"Hi, Nicky," I said as flatly as I could.

"Smelly Fried Egg, how's it going? Where's Pwince Charming, off fighting dragons or something?"

"Let's go," whispered Allie.

I ignored both of them and ordered my cone.

"Hey, what's THAT?" I turned around to see Nicky pointing at O.J.

"That's my practice dog," I informed him.

"Your WHAT?" Nicky aimed a kick at O.J., who I yanked up by his leash just in time. "You think that's a dog? You better get new glasses!"

"No," I told him. "I think it's a plastic jug. But I'm practicing for when I get a real dog. A big one that bites," I added.

"That's the dumbest thing I ever heard!" hooted Nicky.

Just then, someone yelled, "Hey, shrimp!"

Allie and I turned, while Nicky seemed to flinch at the sound of the words. "What?" yelled Nicky at his big brother, who was sitting in the driver's seat of a yellow convertible parked next to the Dairy Barn.

"Be sure they make my milkshake extra-thick!"

"I don't have enough," whined Nicky.

"Just do it," demanded his brother. Nicky scowled back at him but said nothing.

When Allie got her creemee, she followed me over to our favorite picnic table.

"Let's go," she hissed again.

"No," I told her, even though my heart was pounding from what had just happened. We always ate our cones at this table. I wasn't going to let Nicky take that away. Just then, I heard the cashier saying something to Nicky.

"Aw, c'mon, close enough," said Nicky. "Just give me the shake."

"You're ten cents short," said the cashier firmly, shaking her head. When she said the word *short*, I noticed for the first time just how short Nicky actually was. He looked particularly tiny and naked-mole-rat-ish trying to glare over the ice cream counter, which was fairly high up.

Allie smiled with satisfaction. I felt like smiling too. It was great to have a front-row seat for Nicky getting what he deserved. Without really thinking about it, I reached into my pocket and pulled out the change I had left. Shining in my hand was a dime.

I wrapped my fingers around it and lifted my clenched fist high.

"Hey, Nicky," I yelled.

Nicky turned, his eyes narrowed, his mouth pinched into a scowl.

I could already picture Jeremy's wide-mouthed laugh as I replayed the scene for him and described how I got Nicky back for the pennies. I imagined the expression of surprise and alarm that would cross Nicky's face as he saw the coin hurtling toward him. He might even put up his hands and cry out in fear. Come to think of it, he already looked like he might cry.

I lowered my hand. "Catch," I called, tossing him the dime underhand.

"Thanks," he said gruffly, after examining it. He paid and carried the shake back to the car without another word. I noticed he didn't have an ice cream for himself. As the car

pulled away, Nicky looked at me. Not with gratitude or anger. Just confusion. And maybe suspicion, like he wasn't used to people doing nice things for him.

I laughed. I was surprised at how good it felt to show him he didn't get to me.

"What did you do *that* for?" asked Allie.

I shrugged. "Gotta start somewhere," I said.

On the way home, Allie took a turn pulling O.J. "I've always wanted a dog too," she said shyly. "Maybe I should ask my parents if I can get a dog when you get yours."

"That would be so cute! Hey, maybe we could get puppies from the same litter!"

"Yeah! And we could name them something that went together," said Allie.

"Like Apollo and Artemis," I suggested. "Or Ruby and Amethyst."

"Or Bacon and Eggs!"

"No, please," I groaned. "No more breakfast names."

"What? I think that'd be cute," said Allie.

We walked on, planning what our puppies would look like, how we'd get them matching leashes and collars, and where we'd take them on walks together. O.J. lagged behind us on the path, rattling along companionably.

"I really thought you were going to hit him with that coin," said Allie.

"So did I," I admitted, kicking a little stone along the path. I guess sometimes you don't know things about yourself until you do.

CHAPTER 19

Since Ace had his heart attack, my mom has started talking about going to temple to check it out and maybe even to join. I'm still not sure how I feel about the Hebrew school part, but I guess I'm game to give it a try. It might be nice to meet some other Jewish kids, whether or not they live on cherry farms. Unfortunately, I probably won't get to actually go with Jeremy because my mom thinks we'd be more comfortable at the *Star Wars* Shema temple. This makes Jeremy very jealous.

"Look on the bright side," I told him the other day while we were taking a walk. "Maybe your rabbi will figure out a way to sing some other prayer to the theme song from *Malone at Last*." Which was the new Matt Malone movie that was about to open. Jeremy and Allie and I had made plans to go

see it on opening day as sort of a last hurrah before the summer ended and sixth grade began.

"Yeah, sure," said Jeremy, but I could tell from the way he said it that he hoped I was right. "Hey, look out," he added, pointing to a puddle on the sidewalk.

A puddle freshly made . . .

by my new puppy.

That's right, *my dog.*

A real, flesh-and-blood, tail-wagging, stick-fetching (well, not yet, but someday!) dog, which my parents finally agreed to let me get after—and, now that I think about it, maybe *because*—O.J. survived Ace's heart attack.

"No fair!" howled Sam. "How come she gets a dog?"

"Now, Sammy," said my mom. "Your sister has been very diligent about taking care of O.J."

"And," added my dad, "she'll be eleven in a little over a month. So, Zelly, you can consider this an early birthday present."

I picked up my puppy and hugged him tight, just like on the cover of *Shiloh.* I breathed deep, smelling his puppy smell. It was the best smell I ever smelled, even better than the tall grass in the field out behind The Farm. My puppy licked my ear, making me laugh. I set him down in my lap and petted his velvety dark-brown-and-white fur and scratched behind his small, floppy ears. He wagged his whole body with happiness, almost as if he hadn't figured out how to control just his tail yet.

"I guess Ace was right," mused my mom, watching me. "She's ready."

"They always said he was the wisest man in Chelm," said my dad, winking.

"Not just in Chelm," I said. I still couldn't believe Ace had pulled it off, even though the proof was right there in my lap. But somehow he had. Somehow *we* had.

"What kind of dog is he?" asked Sam, still looking a little jealous. He had one hand on his favorite birthday present, the new lightsaber I made for him out of a flashlight, a long cardboard tube, and yellow fluorescent paint. It looked as if he was trying to reassure himself that it was almost as good as a puppy. Both his wrists were covered with rubber bands, which, in some sort of nutty tribute to Ace, he still refused to take off.

"According to the authorities at the Chittenden County Humane Society . . . he's a mutt," said my dad. "Although I think he's mostly English springer spaniel."

"His coloring is called 'liver and white,'" added my mom.

"I'll have you know he is a *Jewish* springer spaniel," called a voice, "and his color is chopped liver on rye."

With that, Ace hobbled determinedly into the living room. Yes, Ace had come home from the hospital. And he had finally given in and started using his cane. He was still working on getting back his energy, not to mention getting back to his old volume level. He seemed different in a lot of ways. Except for the bad jokes way.

My parents laughed. My puppy wriggled around in my

lap, clearly enjoying the attention. I didn't care what anyone said about his breed or his colors. He was all mine, and I was so happy I felt like my heart would burst.

"Thank you," I told my parents. I turned to Ace. "Thank you so much!"

"You should use him in good health," said Ace. Or, I should say, *Grandpa*. Because, true to his word, when Ace came home from the hospital, he actually decided to retire the whole "Ace" business. Whenever it comes up, he makes jokes about how he's trying out new nicknames, like "Czar" or "Emperor" or his favorite, "Grand Pooh-Bah." And if you call him Ace, he waves his hand and frowns. "That guy?" he says. "He's ancient history."

My dad says it won't last. He says that as soon as Grandpa's voice returns, he'll go right back to being the same old Ace. Me, I'm not so sure. Though, in a way, I hope my dad is right. I can't believe it, but I actually miss the old Ace. Almost as much as I miss Bubbles, because as much as I loved Bubbles, she didn't drive me crazy the way Ace did. I guess that's what love is, sometimes. The power to drive you crazy. And to make you do crazy things, like drag an old orange juice jug all over town. Which seems a whole lot less crazy from where I'm sitting: on the floor, with my new puppy in my lap.

"What are you going to name him?" asked my dad.

"O.J., perhaps?" asked my mom.

I shook my head.

I knew just what to name him, and it wasn't O.J.

Not because I don't like the name. It's just that it's a Jewish tradition to name things to honor special people who are no longer with us. Like me being named after my great-aunt Zipporah. And O.J., I'm pleased to say, is still around.

O.J. sits on top of the bookcase in my room, in a place of honor. He's a little dirty, a little dented, but always, always smiling. When I come home from a walk, my new dog curls up in a dog bed right next to my bookcase, and O.J. smiles down

on my new dog,

who

(with my grandpa's blessing)

I named

Ace.

THE END

A GLOSSARY OF YIDDISH WORDS

by Zelda Irene Fried

My grandpa is named Abraham Diamond, and my grandma was named Belle Diamond. A long time ago, when they were kids, their parents and grandparents spoke a language called Yiddish. My grandpa sometimes calls this language "Jewish," which is what *Yiddish* means.

Yiddish is a very, very old language that started as a blend of German, Hebrew, French, Polish, and other languages in the twelfth century or earlier. Yiddish is written using the letters of the Hebrew alphabet. My grandpa says he remembers his father reading Yiddish newspapers in New York when he was a little boy. My dad told me that in Orthodox Jewish communities all over the world, some people still speak, read, and write Yiddish. He showed me online that there's even a Yiddish Book Center in Amherst, Massachusetts. Their purpose is to rescue Yiddish books and share them with the world. They have a huge collection of old Yiddish books, plus new ones too. They even have a book called *Di Kats der Payats*. You know what that is? It's *The Cat in the Hat* in Yiddish, even though "payats" really means "clown."

My grandpa doesn't read or write in Yiddish much

anymore. But he does use a lot of Yiddish words, even when he is speaking English. Like *bagel*. Did you know that was a Yiddish word? Neither did I until my grandpa told me. Here are some more Yiddish words and what they mean:

bubbe – Grandma. My grandma was called "Bubbles" because I got the words *bubbe* and *bubbles* mixed up when I was little.

bubeleh – Little grandma, but people sometimes say it to mean "darling" or "sweetie." You can say it to a man or a woman or a kid.

bupkis – Nothing, or something that is worth nothing. What it actually means is "beans."

chazerai – Junk, but people usually say it to mean "junk food," like candy, especially if there's a lot of it.

Chelm – A mythical town of fools, where the wise man is the biggest fool. My grandma always called my grandpa "the wisest man in Chelm" to tease him.

chutzpah – My mom says this means "nerve." My dad says you say this about someone who does something outrageous. Here is his example: A beggar asks for food, saying he has no money and will pay next week. The baker feels sorry and gives him a dozen bagels. The beggar then points out that the bakery rule is that if you get twelve bagels, you get an extra one free and demands a thirteenth bagel. "That's chutzpah" is what my dad says.

Chutzpah can also mean "courage." For example, it would take a lot of chutzpah to jump in a pond that might have leeches in it.

goy – A person who is not Jewish. More than one are "goyim."

hock – My grandpa says "Stop hocking me" when he means stop bugging him about something. My mom says it actually means "to bang on something," like a gong. So you could say it about someone who talks your ear off, like our neighbor Mrs. Stanley. Only she's really nice, so I wouldn't say it about her, even if it is true.

kvell – To act very proud of something or someone. My grandma used to kvell about things my brother and I did.

kvetch – To complain. My grandpa kvetches about things my brother and I do.

meshuggener – A crazy person. My grandpa yells this at the TV a lot. You can also say that a crazy thing—like a fish that jumps out of the water and into your lap—or a crazy idea is "meshugge."

nosh – To have a snack. It also means "a snack." So you can nosh on a nosh!

nu – This sort of means "so?" or "well?" But my grandpa says, "So, nu?" which seems to me like saying the same thing twice.

oy vey – Oh no! My grandpa also says "Vey iz mir," which is like an "oy vey" times ten.

Shabbes – From Friday night at sundown to Saturday night at sundown is called Shabbes. My mom says in Hebrew it is also called Shabbat, which is the day of rest. When she was growing up, her parents would make a special meal every Friday night and sometimes invite friends and neighbors to join them.

shammes – This means "helper," which is why you call the candle you use to help light the rest of the Chanukah candles "the shammes."

shayna – Beautiful. My grandma called me "shayna punim," which means "beautiful face," and "shayna velt," which means "beautiful world," and sometimes just plain "shayna."

Shema – This is a special Hebrew prayer. My friend Jeremy says the word *shema* means "hear." So the prayer starts "Shema Yisrael," which means "Hear, Israel . . ." But it doesn't mean Israel the country. It's more like "Listen up, all Jewish people . . ." He learned this at Hebrew school, so I guess that must be right.

shiksa – A girl or woman who is not Jewish.

shiva – "Sitting shiva" means "staying home and mourning," usually for seven days ("shiva" means "seven" in Hebrew), after a family member dies. There are lots of rules about sitting shiva. I think one of them is that people who visit have to bring food.

shmeer – A small amount of something you can spread, like a "shmeer" of cream cheese on a bagel.

shmendrick – I think this means "a loser" or "a jerk." I asked my grandpa and he said "A shmendrick means a shmendrick."

shtikl – A small piece of something (the *l* at the end means "little"). My grandma used to say "Nem a shtikl cake" whenever we visited. She meant "Take a little piece of cake."

tuchus – You sit on this. Guess what it is.

zorg zikh nisht – My grandpa says this means "Don't worry about it." But whenever he says it, you *know* there's something to worry about!

ACKNOWLEDGMENTS

I am grateful for the love, support, and encouragement of my family, especially my wonderful husband, Mike, our book- and dog-crazy daughters, Franny and Bougie, and our devoted dog, Lucy. I am also thankful for my terrific friends—I hope you guys will forgive me for not listing each and every one of you—who've always been there for me. Especially helpful to this book were Mary Kay Zuravleff; Katy Kelly; Susan Shreve and Tim Seldes (and their dogs: Zelda, Miss Elly, and Kubla, respectively); my amazing agent, Carrie Hannigan; and the Virginia Center for the Creative Arts. Erin Clarke and everyone at Knopf Books for Young Readers have my eternal gratitude for reading, loving, and championing this book. And special thanks go to Dan and Elly Perl and John and Maryann Sewell, four of the grandest parents (and best grandparents) anyone could be lucky enough to have.

Extra-large creemees of appreciation must be provided to my Vermont crew. They include: Anais Langley, Amy Halverson, Maria Lee, Kate Charron, Milia Bell, and Jennifer Spafford Danish (collectively known as the HC86); Greg and Jena Strong; my beloved BuFTY buddies, especially Eric Slesar; my fabulous cousin Bari Nan Cohen; and my Green

Mountain PR Machine, Lisa Schamberg. Hugs and knishes go to the Dream Team that vetted my Yiddishisms: Maxwell "Mac" Postow (my great-uncle, who at ninety-eight is easily one of the coolest people I know), Emily Perl Kingsley (my aunt, who is younger than Uncle Mac, but no less excellent), my parents, and the copyediting mensches at Knopf.

The character of Ace was inspired by my grandfather Alan Francis Perl, who died in December 2002. It was also shaped by the relationship I was fortunate enough to have with all my grandparents (including the rubber band queen, Miriam "Dearie" Postow, who is still with us), and two of my great-grandparents, for the better part of my childhood. Like Ace, Grandpa Alan was a dedicated fisherman, golfer, and Trekkie. He was also an enthusiastic collector of odd tchotchkes and bad jokes, and an inveterate arguer. The world misses him. As do I.

ABOUT THE AUTHOR

Erica S. Perl is the author of many celebrated children's books, including *Dotty, Chicken Butt!*, and *Chicken Bedtime Is Really Early*. She is also the author of the young adult novel *Vintage Veronica*. Erica was raised in Burlington, Vermont, by transplanted New Yorkers. She is happy to report that you can now get excellent bagels in the Green Mountain State. Erica currently lives in Washington, D.C., with her husband, two daughters, and, of course, a dog. Her website is ericaperl.com.